face **relations**

race relations

face **relations**

11
stories
about
seeing
beyond color

edited by
MARILYN SINGER

Simon & Schuster Books for Young Readers
New York   London   Toronto   Sydney

SIMON & SCHUSTER BOOKS FOR YOUNG READERS
An imprint of Simon & Schuster Children's Publishing Division
1230 Avenue of the Americas, New York, New York 10020

Book design by Lucy Ruth Cummins
The text for this book is set in Rotis Serif.
Manufactured in the United States of America

10 9 8 7 6 5 4 3 2 1

Library of Congress Cataloging-in-Publication Data
Face relations : 11 stories about seeing beyond color / edited by
Marilyn Singer.
p. cm.
ISBN 0-689-85637-7
1. Short stories, American. [1. Interpersonal relations—Fiction.
2. Short stories.] I. Singer, Marilyn.
PZ5 .A248 2004
[Fic]—dc21   2003008840

To Possibilities

Many thanks to all the people who gave sage advice, especially Jennifer Armstrong, Steve Aronson, Michael Cart, Michele Coppola, Kathleen Cotter, Michelle Gahee, Yasmin Gallop, Kelly Milner Halls, Stacy Leigh, David Lubar, Joe Morton, David Mowery, Karrie Myers, Ernie Porcelli, Rebecca Porcelli, and Dian Curtis Regan; to my wonderful editors, David Gale and Ellia Bisker and the S&S crew; and to the incredible writers whose work in this book I've had the pleasure of editing.

CONTENTS

INTRODUCTION

I confess: I've been a *Star Trek* fan for years. I've watched every episode of every series, some more than once. The sight of the Enterprise, with its multiethnic, multiracial, multi-species crew, still fills me with hope.

But you don't have to be a Trekker to believe that we humans can learn to live with and value each other. One day I heard someone on the radio say that he felt "honored" to ride the New York City subways with people of so many heritages. I try to invoke that privilege even when I'm squished between hordes of commuters on the rush-hour Q train. Sometimes it works. Sometimes it doesn't. My goal is to keep trying.

I believe we *all* should keep trying to acknowledge, appreciate, and celebrate our diversity. But I've lived long enough—and in probably the most diverse city in the world—to know that this is seldom easy. Every day we have to uncover, examine, and fight the prejudices we've acquired, usually from early childhood on. Anyone who thinks we've eliminated racism and bigotry in the twenty-first century is asleep at the wheel. Racism—the widespread system of advantage based on race—is, unfortunately, still with us. So is bigotry—prejudice based on race, creed, sex, etc. We have to struggle daily against feelings of fear and powerlessness, inertia, group pressure, and the constant bombardment of negative stereotypes, both obvious and subtle, to change ourselves, and others, too. Which brings me to this book.

Face Relations: 11 Stories About Seeing Beyond Color is not a book about prejudice (although prejudice is most certainly an important part of this book). It is about the possibilities of embracing diversity. With naivete, ambivalence, intent, anger, fear, embarrassment, and joy, the characters in these stories tear down the barriers that separate us.

In Jess Mowry's "Phat Acceptance," meet Brandon, a guy with that cool white surfer-dude look—even if he isn't a surfer— whose first day in a new school is turned upside down by the arrival of the one, the only, the *fattest* black classmate he's ever seen. And there's Mitch, narrator of Joseph Bruchac's "Skins," a football player of Native American and Scandinavian heritage, whose strategy of "hanging back" is challenged by the two new kids in town: Randolph, clearly African-American, and Jimmy T, purely American Indian. Or are they?

Get to know DeMaris—pining for her best friend Epiphany, the title character in Ellen Wittlinger's story—who dares to ask: Why can't a white girl sit with the black kids in the cafeteria? In Noelle's school, some of the *black* kids aren't allowed to sit with the black kids. Sherri Winston, in her story "Snow," introduces us to this budding journalist whose fight against the mistreatment of Haitian students by fellow African-American classmates leads her to a dangerous clash with the school principal.

Kyoko Mori's protagonist in "Black and White" tells the story of an "outsider" from an immigrant's own perspective. Born in Japan and growing up in rural Wisconsin, Asako learns that being the misunderstood "foreigner" doesn't excuse her act of mean-spirited Halloween vandalism.

Then there are Jemma, also an immigrant, in Marina Budhos's "Gold," and Bianca, living amid immigrants, in M. E. Kerr's "Hearing Flower." One is biracial and poor, the other rich and white, but each has suffered the loss of a parent and each is in love with the "wrong" boy.

At least these boys are the right age. What are we to make of Myra with a thing for her math teacher, Rita Williams-Garcia's "Mr. Ruben." No one can tell what race Mr. Ruben is. But poor Myra, she just *can't* have a crush on the man unless he's black—and she'll drive herself and her friend Dee crazy until she finds out if he is or not.

Myra's situation makes us laugh. PD's does not. He was a promising Latino trumpet player. Now, he's dead. But oh, what he's left behind! René Saldaña Jr.'s moving story "The Heartbeat of the Soul of the World" is about PD's legacy—and the unifying power of music.

A very different soul hovers over Beth and Vonny in my own story "Negress"—the ghost of Saartjie Baartman, the Hottentot Venus, a woman exhibited as a sexual freak throughout Europe in the early nineteenth century. Will her spirit unite or divide these two very different best friends? What possibilities does she have in store for them?

In Naomi Shihab Nye's "Hum," Sami is haunted by spirits too—spirits of the dead and the living he left behind in the Middle East. But he and his family are hopeful about their new life in Texas. And then comes the day that changes everything: September 11, 2001.

These characters'—these writers'—stories are troubled, sad, touching, funny, or fierce, but all are full of hope. And if hope really is, in Emily Dickinson's words, "the thing with feathers / That perches in the soul / And sings the tune without the words / And never stops at all," may these stories supply some possible lyrics. May you hear their words and music long after you close this book.

Marilyn Singer

Every day, classrooms have the potential to transform impressionable hearts and excited minds into engines for change, innovation, and leadership. Teaching Tolerance, a project of the Southern Poverty Law Center, has worked for more than ten years to support teachers, principals, and parents as they prepare today's children to live in a nation that looks much different than it did even a few years ago.

Tolerance, we believe, is a personal decision that every person on earth is a treasure, and as such, is entitled to live in welcoming communities, to learn in safe schools, and to work in environments that allow them an equal opportunity to excel. Tolerance is the most American of our values, and demands we all play a role in creating just and fair communities.

Because of the commitment of our supporters and the creativity of our staff, the SPLC has been able to provide free diversity education resources to hundreds of thousands of educators. From an award-winning magazine, to our interactive Web site, to video and text kits that have garnered Academy Award recognition, Teaching Tolerance is at the forefront, equipping youth with the skills they will need to flourish in the rapidly diversifying communities in our country.

In pursuit of that goal, we continue to press for innovative ideas. For instance, our national Mix It Up at Lunch Day campaign encourages all of us to take a look at our surroundings. What unwritten rules limit our ability to enjoy new experiences, explore new cultures, and to make new friends? Once you identify those rules, break them.

Ask yourself two questions: What kind of community do

you want to live in, and what are you willing to do to make it a reality?

Today turn exactly six months ahead in your calendar. Write down one thing you will do to change your community. When that date arrives, ask yourself "Did I do what I said I would?" If you have, celebrate. If you have not, recommit yourself to doing it.

For more information about Teaching Tolerance and the Southern Poverty Law Center, visit our Web site at www.tolerance.org. There you can find details about how to help promote tolerance in your community. It is our responsibility to create a stronger America than we inherited, and together we can.

Thank you to the writers who contributed stories to this collection and to Simon & Schuster for publishing them.

Kelvin Datcher
Outreach Director
Southern Poverty Law Center
www.splcenter.org

face **relations**

PHAT

ACCEPTANCE

by Jess Mowry

Maybe he wasn't the world's fattest kid, but he was definitely the fattest that Brandon had seen. He wasn't the only fat kid in the house; of the thirty-two freshmen in history class, at least eight were packing extra pounds, from a little bit chubby to totally huge, but this boy was off the fat grading scale!

Brandon tried not to stare at the dude, though he'd chosen a desk at the rear of the room *because* he wanted to watch everybody. His creative writing teacher last year had said that a good writer had to "observe," but so far here on this first day of school, in these opening minutes of history class, there hadn't been a lot to observe that might have inspired an original story. The kids were a typical Santa Cruz mix—meaning that most of them were white—from surfers in tank tops, hoodies, and shorts to hip-hops in big-jeans and backward-turned caps. A pair of gothics, boy and girl, had so many piercings that Brandon winced, even though he was wearing an earring himself. There were also a couple of obvious jocks.

Two surfers were tanned to the shade of old pennies. One

could have starred in *Endless Summer,* a buff-bodied blond dude with bottle-bleached locks, while the other resembled a wiry coyote, his torso as hard as a sheet-metal roof. The third was as brown as an Indian boy, which made a dramatic contrast to his hair, a multihued mix of the palest shades that couldn't have come in a home tinting kit. He was also a big-bellied, baby-fat dude who looked like he'd just spent the night on a beach, with sand in his hair and beer on his breath.

The goths were as pale as vanilla ice cream and as bony as week-old cadavers. One of the hip-hops was borderline chubby, though hiding it well in his oversize clothes, while one of the jocks could have been on TV as a model for all-American boys. There was also a skinhead in boots and suspenders who could have passed for an albino ape, though the only "statement" he seemed to make was that some Caucasians had lame-looking skulls and should have kept something on top of them. Of the ten other white kids, Brandon included, most were more or less average in build, with a couple of girls who were "pleasingly plump" and one who resembled a Barbie doll, which looked almost scary in real life. At a desk in the front sat a marshmallow dude with a belly as big as the Goodyear blimp. He might have been shy about showing it off, though he seemed really proud of a souvenir shirt—I SAW AREA 51!—in spite of its being three sizes too small.

The other students included three Asians, two slender girls who were Vietnamese, and a Japanese boy in a camouflage shirt with a screaming pattern of yellow and orange. Four kids were brown, and three of them fat: a raven-haired girl with a dazzling smile and a pair of chubby Mexican boys in tattered white T-shirts and faded big-jeans. The other

2

brown girl might have been Middle Eastern. The black race hadn't been represented, until this ebony mountain of blubber had lumbered casually into the room.

That wasn't a good description, thought Brandon; an author had to portray his people so readers could picture them clearly. For one thing, mountains didn't "lumber"; and this dude was nothing but wobbly rolls, his chest a pair of water balloons and his waist resembling a truck tire tube like those you could rent at the Boardwalk. His clothes were kind of carelessly cool: a black T-shirt, at least triple-X, though it still couldn't cover his titanic tummy—along with an old pair of gangster jeans that gave a new meaning to "saggers." Their cuffs dragged the floor over big bulky boots, which seemed to go well with his bulldozer size.

Brandon made notes in his "writer's journal," a section reserved in his shiny new binder. At least this dude was something new, and a prime candidate for his "Beastworld" book, a graphic novel he planned to write as soon as he found an illustrator. He realized he was staring again, not being "detached" like a writer should be. He shifted his eyes from all that loose lard and raised them instead to the fat boy's face, which made him think of an African cherub: chubby round cheeks, a wide button nose, and eyes like shiny obsidian. His big white teeth were partly displayed in a comfortable kind of perpetual grin, while his hair resembled a lion's mane that tumbled over his brawny shoulders and midway down his massive back. It might have been braided, or maybe dreadlocked, though Brandon wasn't exactly sure, not being down with African culture. He guessed it was only logical that the boy was coming in his direction, his huge belly clearing a road ahead as kids leaned aside to get out of his way.

The desks were arranged in five rows of six, with another four at the rear of the room, and Brandon sat in the back right corner, the farthest away from the door. The desk to his left was unoccupied, while the chubby surfer sat sprawled in the third, scenting the air with his alcohol fumes and shedding a virtual beach on the floor. Brandon had made a few notes about him—his hoodie unbuttoned, a sneaker untied, his hair in a tangle of salt-stiffened curls that almost completely concealed his eyes. One of the white girls, an "average type," sat in the fourth desk beside the surfer, and wasn't looking too stoked about it. There was another available desk in the very first row at the front of the room, but any cool kid would have naturally chosen the less conspicuous one at the rear, and taken their chances on Brandon.

Brandon was cool enough, he supposed, though a little detached from the center of cool. If cool was a sun, then he was a planet, not shining himself but reflecting the rays. At age fourteen he was average height, with silky blond hair, in a central part, that flowed down over his chest and back like a feral young prince in a sorcery game. His eyes were bright blue, his nose a bit snubbed; his lips often rested partly open to show off a pair of large front teeth. He had a few muscles in all the right places; his chest was high and gently defined, though his tummy was still a bit round like a child's, which tended to give him a Bugs Bunny look. He'd tried working out with his big brother's weights, but had only developed a killer backache. A chiropractor had aligned his spine—beneath the eyes of his worried mother—while scolding him for being "brainwashed" and falling for "that ideal image that Hollywood shoves at American kids."

Still, Brandon managed to look pretty cool: His tan was as deep as the drunk surfer-boy's, and he'd carefully chosen his clothes this morning to give him a sort of indifferent pose—a blue denim shirt from his brother's collection with three buttons open to show off his chest, along with an old pair of loose Tommy jeans and experienced-looking skater sneaks. Most Santa Cruz kids would have thought him a surfer—the drunk boy had dreamily greeted him, "Duuuude"—a cool enough image to have in this town. It was also a look that didn't offend or attract any special attention: good camouflage to be an observer without getting caught in a mix.

The mammoth black boy was grinning at Brandon as if he'd been reading his mind. Obsidian eyes queried Brandon's blue, confirming the desk was available. Brandon tried to control his stare, but the boy was just so awesomely . . . FAT! Brandon glanced around again to observe the other kids' reactions.

The average white girl abandoned her desk, not wanting to sit with an unrated Brandon, a drunk and smelly surfer-dude, and now this enormous ebony boy. She snatched her things and fled to the front, landing beside the Area 51 kid. The other two surfers were smirking now. The all-American looked disgusted. The skinhead was beaming a stupid hate stare that he probably practiced every morning while scraping the fuzz off his simian skull. The 51 kid seemed a little relieved at no longer being the fattest in class, while the Mexican dudes might have been impressed, and the Japanese boy was scanning the black guy as if thinking of sumo wrestlers. Most of the girls wore a mix of expressions, which seemed to range from amazement to pity, with maybe a flicker of interest or two. A few of the kids looked a little confused, as if they didn't know how to react: There weren't many black dudes in Santa Cruz, and nobody knew much about them. Their movies and music were freezer burn cool, and Brandon had heard all the usual stories about how strong and bad they were. But this dude didn't fit into his role any more than his clothes fit him.

Then Brandon wondered how *he* should react. The other students were watching *him,* too. He felt as if he was up on a stage and no one had told him what part to play. This massive black boy was invading his space on the very first day of *high school,* dammit! It felt like his cool was a house of cards and this woolly black mammoth was shaking the floor. Brandon had gone to a private school from kindergarten through junior high, so he didn't know anyone here. He had no posse to take his back and validate his coolness permit. He remembered something his father had said about making career decisions. Nobody would dis him for dissing this dude, but they'd probably dis him for not. And they'd have him under a microscope for all this freakin' period. Observer, hell! he told himself; *he* was the one who was being observed, scanned, filed and categorized, labeled and tagged for the next four years by how he treated this huge black kid within the next forty minutes!

He turned for support to the sandy surfer, who sprawled with sockless sneaks splayed out, his sloppy body mostly bare in a sleeveless hoodie and old cutoff jeans. He wore a charm around his neck, a sort of wooden tiki god that dangled from a leather strip between a pair of bobby shapes that could have passed for breasts. His eyes were lost beneath his hair, that messy mass of tangled locks, bleached by years of sun and salt

Jess Mowry

and clearly never combed. A rat was tattooed on one of his arms above a chubby biceps muscle, a Disney kind of cartoon rat who grinned around a big cigar, the sort of thing a kid would love but most adults would hate. Two words were tattooed underneath, but Brandon couldn't read them without getting close and personal, and since he didn't know the dude, he hadn't dared to try. But any boy who had a tat would naturally be cool, and his judgment would be final in this freshman student court. . . .

But, dammit, he was sleeping!

The mammoth black kid reached the desk. Brandon almost expected the hiss of air brakes. The dude shed his pack and his shirt rose high as he wiggled out of the straining straps, revealing a funnel-like cave of a navel that tunneled away into darkness. Brandon scanned the surfer-boy, still hoping for a backup, but the dude was lost in space somewhere, or maybe riding waves. Brandon felt a bit betrayed, yet there was nothing he could do but smile and say, "What's goin' on?" and hope that sounded cool.

Total silence ruled the room. Every ear was listening. The place was like a pack of raptors massing for attack. But, could the prey defend itself? The dude didn't look like a video thug, but his size was still intimidating. Brandon could almost hear the thoughts: Maybe a senior who'd flunked the course and had to take it over again? And who the hell was that other dude? Another surfer-boy? He had the tan, he had the look . . . could possibly be cool.

Snickers were stored away for the moment, and smirks were carefully hidden. Insults waited, locked and loaded, but who would be the first to fire?

The goths looked oddly understanding. The jocks just looked disgusted. The skinhead chewed on broken glass and didn't seem to like the taste. The brown boys traded Latin glances cryptic to Caucasians, and the Anglos seemed to have realized that four of them were overweight, and one of those a surfer.

"Chillin'," said the black dude. "S'up with you?"

"... Oh ... phat," said Brandon, the first "black thing" that came to mind. As soon as it was out of his mouth he felt his cheeks burn red. "I mean with a *p*," he added, sweating. "You know? Like, phat as in cool?"

He really expected a crushing "Duh," but the black boy only chuckled. "I heard it, man."

Then the bell rang and the teacher came in. The other kids turned to check him out ... but they would *remember* that Brandon had smiled and spoken first to the ebony dude. The enormous boy sat down at his desk, and Brandon watched in fascination.

The dude almost had to put the desk *on,* like donning a piece of sports equipment. This took a lot of puffing and struggle. Brandon actually held his breath, wanting to help but not knowing how. He expected the desk to collapse any second and dump the huge kid on the floor. *That* would murder Brandon's cool faster than a cluster bomb! But somehow the structure held together, and the boy finally managed to squeeze into place. Most of his midnight middle was bare, as well as his gigantic bottom. His chest almost covered the desktop, and Brandon wondered how he could write. No one seemed to have seen the show, which Brandon decided was fortunate, both for himself and the titanic dude; the kids were

Jess Mowry

watching the teacher now and probably scanning for weaknesses. The teacher, Mr. Rosenberg, had tactfully chosen not to watch. In fact, he might have distracted the class on purpose by squeakily chalking his name on the board.

"Um?" whispered Brandon. "Are you okay?" Then his cheeks got red again: Had he just said something else uncool?

The fat boy only flashed his grin. "Guess I can wait forty minutes to breathe. Figured the desks would be bigger in high school."

"Yeah," agreed Brandon. "Would've thought so, huh? . . . Um, do you need anything from your pack?" It was clear that the boy couldn't reach his stuff; there was just too much of him to reach over.

"Sure, dawg. Snag me a pen an' the binder."

Brandon flicked a glance at the teacher, who had turned from the board to observe his new class. He looked to be in his middle forties and obviously knew about animal taming. He also acted pretty cool, not seeming to notice when Brandon rose to get the fat boy's things. The binder was ancient and sadly battered but covered with kickin' grafitti cartoons. The dude offered Brandon a big chubby paw. "Travis," he said, guiding Brandon's hand through one of those black—or maybe gang—shakes.

Brandon suddenly realized he had never touched black skin before. What a stupid thing to think! Like, what was it going to do, rub off? "Brandon," said Brandon. "Um, did you draw all this stuff?" he added. "Those toons are really killer."

"Yeah. Thanks, man," the boy replied. "Just a little thing I do."

Mr. Rosenberg cleared his throat, and Brandon scuttled back to his desk. A couple of kids looked over their shoulders, but nobody seemed very interested now.

The teacher flipped open a folder and smiled. "Good morning, ladies and gentlemen, and welcome to World History. Which, believe it or not, you're a part of."

The skinhead raised his hand. "Are we gonna learn about Aryans? Or just that 'multicultural' crap?"

The jocks and surfers snickered a bit, but with him or *at* him was hard to tell. The Area 51 kid seemed a little embarrassed, maybe for the sins of his race, which the skinhead seemed to represent, while the brown boys scowled at one another though otherwise didn't react. Brandon scanned for Travis's view, but the fat boy was only looking amused, as if a baby had said a bad word.

Mr. Rosenberg's smile didn't change. "This is *World History*, Mr. . . . ?"

"Uh, Slater," said the skinhead.

"Joe Slater?"

"Yeah. It's an Aryan name."

"Anglo-Saxon, actually. A mender of roofs—'slates'—you know? But a perfectly honorable occupation." Mr. Rosenberg marked the roll. "Unfortunately, we live in a state which is fiftieth place in the quality of its public education . . . *last* place in the entire country, despite it being the richest. We have many fine new prisons—but prisons, I'm told, make a profit, while we don't have the funding for 'frills' in our schools, such as music, art, and up-to-date books . . . or a special class in European history. However, I think you ought to know that there never was an Aryan race. If you want to study 'Aryans,' you'll need to focus on languages . . . and at your own expense, I'm afraid."

The skinhead's skull flushed neon pink. "That's a . . . not true! I got a book!" He frantically dug in his pack.

"Ah, yes, I'm familiar with *that* one. I've also read *Mein Kampf*. However, Mr. Slater, it's either 'true,' or there have been many other books written—by genuine scholars—for the sole purpose of deceiving you. But I'll be happy to give extra credit for a well-researched paper on Aryans."

Some of the kids looked curious. Joe just looked confused.

The teacher glanced back at his folder. "Please answer up as I read your names. And correct me if I mispronounce."

"Whoa," whispered Brandon to Travis. "I didn't know that. About Aryans."

"I did," said Travis. "Never were any. Just a language . . . Want me to wake up your homie?"

"Um . . . sure," said Brandon. This didn't seem like the time to explain that he didn't know the surfer-dude.

Travis's desk creaked ominously as he leaned way over, reached out with his pen, and tapped the surfer's rolly shoulder. The boy woke up and shook back his hair, scattering sand like a blizzard. "Huh?" he murmured. His eyes were blue, and widened fast. "Whooooa!" he breathed. "Are you ever *fat*!"

He didn't say it loudly, but it drew a few snickers here and there—and also a frown from the teacher.

"You ain't no bone-bag yourself," observed Travis.

The surfer-boy looked around the room, seeming surprised to wake up in school, as if it was some sort of nightmare. He may have still been half asleep, or probably more than slightly drunk, but he had a sort of dreamy face and might have always looked that way. His teeth were big and beaverlike, and his hair fell over his eyes again. Then he smiled and slapped his stomach, which quivered all over like pudding. "Are we ever brothers or what?"

"I think I know what you done last summer," said Travis.

"Yeah, heh," said the boy. "Been totally heliotropic, man." Then he searched the floor at his feet. "Aw, suck! Musta left my stuff at the beach!"

"Um," whispered Brandon, trying to see around Travis's bulk and feeling a little left out. "I've got an extra pen. And tons of pape—" He suddenly became aware that silence ruled the room again, and Mr. Rosenberg was frowning.

"I seem to have a 'Bosco Donatello' penciled in here," said the teacher, regarding his folder curiously, as if someone had played a joke. "Where might this gentleman be? . . . Or not?"

"Oh, heh," said the surfer-boy. "Yo, teacher-dude."

A few kids promptly snickered, but the other surfers seemed surprised and turned to stare at Bosco.

"Thank you . . . dude," replied the teacher, and went on reading names. "Travis White" also got snickers, being sort of an oxymoron, but "Brandon Williams" got nothing at all, not being ethnic or anything special.

Well, thought Brandon, at least one of his teachers was cool, but he had to survive the rest of the day. Which seemed like a walk through a minefield. He'd almost stepped on a mine already, but surfer Bosco had saved his butt, had taken his back by talking to Travis, which gave them both a bonus point.

Mr. Rosenberg closed the folder and roamed the room with his eyes. "I'm not going to alter your seating arrangements; I'll leave that up to you for now . . . unless there's an obvious problem. But I hope it won't be a case of 'Why Are All the Black Kids Sitting Together in the Cafeteria?' That would be history repeating itself, and those who don't learn from history are always doomed to repeat it."

Brandon felt embarrassed for Travis, as if the teacher had singled him out, but Travis only smiled.

"Mr. Tanaka?" added the teacher, turning to the Japanese boy. "Would you please pass out the textbooks?"

The next few minutes were normal enough, with Mr. Rosenberg sketching the course while Tiger Tanaka distributed books. If someone had snickered at Tiger's name, Brandon must have missed it. He slid from his desk to give Bosco some paper and one of his extra Pilot pens. Bosco thought the pen was "boss," like something he'd never seen before, and started drawing a rat on a surfboard. Mr. Rosenberg noticed Brandon, but seemed to approve of his charity.

"You surf, dude?" asked Bosco. "You got the look."

"Nah," said Brandon, who was using this opportunity to read the words on Bosco's arm: TOLA RATS, whatever they were. "But, um, I hang at the Boardwalk a lot. And I usually skateboard every day."

"Skateboards are cool. I got one myself, a classic ol' steel-wheeler. But you oughta check out surfin', man. Ain't nothin' so boss in the whole universe. Not even sex, heh—'less it's havin' it in the ocean."

Brandon considered that picture, then shrugged. "I'm probably too old to learn."

"Nah. I could teach you easy, man. 'Specially if you ride a skate."

"But surfing looks really hard."

"Nah. Cement, now *that's* hard." Bosco turned to Travis. "How 'bout you, big black kahuna?"

Brandon winced, but Travis chuckled. "I can float really good."

"Um?" asked Brandon. "Does it ever bother you, being so black?"

"Huh?" asked Travis and Bosco together.

Brandon's cheeks flushed red again. "I . . . mean fat," he stammered.

Travis smiled. "Somebody's Freudian slip is showin'."

"Huh?" said Bosco.

"Sorry," said Brandon.

"It ain't all bad," said Travis, patting his belly, which rippled in waves. "Bet you can't do this."

"I can," said Bosco. "Just not as much."

"Oh," said Brandon.

"Yo," said Bosco. "You'd be a natural longboarder, man. I got me some big ol' beauties at home just dyin' to meet a dude like you."

"I never heard of black surfers," Travis said, then glanced at Brandon. "Or fat ones either."

"Guess you never been to Hawaii," said Bosco. "An' it wasn't white people who invented surfin'."

"Mmm," said Travis. "You got that right."

"Cool tat," offered Brandon.

"Thanks, dude," said Bosco. "Got it when I was eight. . . . Oh, an' thanks for the paper, too."

Brandon was about to ask about "Tola Rats" when Bosco exclaimed, "Aw, suck! I don't got my schedule! It's back on the beach with my stuff. . . . I guess."

"Suck," agreed Brandon.

"Hey, can I borrow yours, Brandy-boy?"

"Um . . . but I need it myself. I don't even know where the rooms are yet."

"Well . . . like, could you copy it down for me?"

"Planet Earth callin'," said Travis. "It's *his* schedule, man. What good it gonna do you?"

"Oh, yeah."

"What are your classes?" asked Brandon.

Bosco shook more sand from his hair. ". . . Well . . . the regular kind, I guess . . . like, um, history . . ."

"We're *in* history," said Brandon.

"Oh, yeah."

"Yo," said Travis. "Just axe if you can go to the office. They gotta have a copy of your schedule."

"Gentlemen and dudes," said the teacher, materializing suddenly. "I'm glad to see the races and"—he glanced at Bosco—"*other* species mingling. But, I must ask the question: Do we have a problem?"

"Oh, heh," said Bosco. "No prob at all, Mr. . . . um . . . ?"

"It's on the blackboard, Mr. Donatello."

"Oh, yeah. I can see it from here."

"Um," said Brandon. "He lost his schedule."

"I'm sure it's wherever his mind is. . . . Come up to my desk. I'll give you a pass."

"Whoa!" said Bosco after the teacher walked away. "He's kinda cool, huh?"

"Yeah," said Travis. "An' your ass be lucky."

Bosco got up, swaying dangerously, and Brandon grabbed his shoulders.

"Heh," said Bosco, blowing beer fumes in Brandon's face.

"I'm still kinda buzzed. Back-to-school party. I can't remember nothin' last night."

"Did you have sex in the ocean?" asked Travis.

"I think I woulda remembered that."

"Well, pull up your pants 'fore y'all get arrested."

"Oh. Heh. These are my lucky cutoffs, man. But they got kinda small this summer."

"Now we know you a natural blond. . . . Funny, you don't look Italian."

"A lot of Northern Italians are blond. But people always ask me that."

"Learn somethin' new every day," said Travis.

Bosco ambled away, shedding a trail of sand behind him. The other surfers flashed "hang loose" signs, which Bosco returned with a careless smile. Then the coyote surfer turned around.

"I didn't know that was *him,* man!"

"He used to be a collie before he got run over," said Travis.

"You mean Bosco?" asked Brandon.

"He won the Pacific championship! On a freakin' ten-footer antique, dude! But he kinda does his own thing," said the surfer.

"Oh," said Brandon. "That sounds like him."

"You dudes doin' anything for lunch?"

"We'll pencil you in," said Travis.

"Sweet."

Brandon sat down and whispered to Travis, "I hope we have some more classes together."

"Yeah," agreed Travis. "That would be cool. I don't know anybody yet. Just moved down here from Oakland this summer."

"I don't know anybody either," said Brandon. "Went to another school." He glanced to the doorway as Bosco left. "He's kind of a mess. But a cool kind of mess."

Travis smiled. "Phattest dude on the planet."

by Joseph Bruchac

The first day I saw Jimmy T. Black, I thought he was a real
Indian. Realer than me. I thought that even before I heard him
tell the group of kids hanging around him that his middle ini-
tial stood for "Thorpe." Jim Thorpe was the Sac and Fox guy
who won the Olympics about a century ago and was the
world's greatest athlete, which I know not just from reading
about him (although I do more reading than any other kid in
Long Pond High), but also almost firsthand.

    You see, I'd heard a bunch of Jim Thorpe stories from Uncle
Tommy Fox, who is eighty-four years old and has packed more
living into his life than most people could experience in three
centuries. Uncle Tommy knew the real Jim Thorpe. He met him
back in 1937 when Uncle Tommy went to Hollywood as a kid
and got lots of bit parts as Anonymous Indian Number Two or
Three who spectacularly falls off his horse when the fair-haired
cowboy hero fires his six-shooter at the attacking horde of
bloodthirsty redskins, who seem to attract fatal bullets like
magnets do iron filings.

But this story isn't actually about Uncle Tommy, even though he is sort of part of it. This all happened the autumn when Uncle Tommy was away visiting his daughter and his grandchildren out in New Mexico. So I should get back to Jimmy T and also our high school, which is, of course, where I first met him.

Long Pond Central High School is pretty big for the North Country. Its being a central school means it draws in students from all the little towns and hamlets around what we laughingly call the major population center of Long Pond. Long Pond High is big enough to have eleven-man football. That is an achievement. Before our central school was built two decades ago, some of the little regional high schools could barely scrape together a five-guy basketball team. Since we have a hundred seniors, and even more kids in our junior class, we have the whole range of sports. Football, basketball, wrestling, hockey, baseball, track, girls' softball, and girls' basketball. And because there's not much else around to do at nights—which get mucho long in the autumn and the winter— we always get big crowds at all our sporting events.

When you go to a high school in a town so small that you have to look twice to see it when you're passing through, everyone knows who you are. I don't mean they know your name and your face. I mean they know everything about you, including the things you wish they'd forget. Memory is, so to speak, a female dog. That is how Uncle Tommy puts it. I don't think he could swear if he wanted to, but he always gets his point across.

Anyhow, as I said, everyone knows who you are. That's

especially true in school, where you've been with the same kids ever since you were in preschool together. As a result, they remember the time when you were five and you got yelled at by the teacher and expelled for a week because you bit a certain girl in the butt so hard that you left tooth marks. Another thing everyone remembers about me is my hair. It is long now and black as Jimmy T's; I have it back in a ponytail. But I know that everyone in school remembers that until sixth grade my hair was kind of a dirty brown. That is what happens when your father was an Indian but your mom is Scandinavian and as blond as Brunhilde. Despite the hair coloring that I comb in every week or so, I know that my classmates still see the old Mitchell Sabattis, would-be Native American. And even though I tan up real dark in the summer, my skin still gets as pale as something you might find under a rock during the winter.

Summer, by the way, is short up here. It's the shortest of our three actual seasons, which go by various names. (You can forget about spring—some years it doesn't even bother to visit.) Old-timers say the year here is broken up into Black Fly Season, Mosquito Season, and Thank God They're Gone. Diehard Northern sports fans and the jocks, though, know that our three big seasons are Football, Basketball, and Off. Of course, for the flatlanders who flock here as tourists, the three seasons are Fishing, Hunting, and Snowmobiling. Although there are still some locals who work in the woods, the pulp and paper industries just aren't what they used to be up here anymore. So the biggest industry—much as we make fun of it—is tourism.

I think I know a million tourist jokes, half of them about

Joseph Bruchac

hunters from the city, who are, after all, just tourists in loud suits with guns. Like the one about the flatland hunter who shot his friend by accident and then dragged him ten miles through the woods to the Long Pond Hospital Emergency Room. Finally, after hours of surgery, the doctor comes out to tell the man that his friend didn't make it, then the doctor says, "You know, he would have had a better chance if you hadn't gutted him out before you brought him in."

Anyhow, it was tourism that brought the four new kids to our school that autumn, Jim Thorpe Black among them. Their parents all moved here because of the Long Pond Northern Adirondack Interpretive Center that opened this year. When new kids come to a community as tight-knit as Long Pond, it makes waves. The fact that we were getting no fewer than four new kids in our high school this year hit us like a tsunami. (In case you do not know, a tsunami is a giant tidal wave probably caused by an underwater earthquake. I was banned for life from all Trivial Pursuit games by my friends because no one else could ever win when I played.)

When new kids come to a high school, there's two ways it can go. One way is that everybody tries to get to know them. The other way is that everybody just hangs back and watches to see what they're like before making a move.

With Jimmy T it was approach numero uno all the way. Word had gotten out that the new kid was a star quarterback. Maybe it was Coach who first mentioned it, at one of our preseason practices. Or maybe it was just that strange telepathic grapevine that every school seems to have. Anyway, the buzz about Jimmy T had gone around. He'd been all-league last year as a junior in a big city school; scouts from Notre Dame and

Syracuse were already checking him out. After decades of our being in the cellar, the doormats for the whole North Country league, this football season might be different. That might not mean much to you, but that's because you never went to a school like ours. The idea of someone leading us out of the wilderness to a winning season was like divine intervention. A good quarterback was like Moses and Eminem rolled up into one. Long Pond kids flocked around Jimmy T the way bees swarm around honey. There he was with that long black hair, olive skin, and shiny white teeth. He was graceful in the way he moved, and he had the stage presence of a pop idol.

"Doesn't he look like Enrique Iglesias?" one girl whispered to another as they pushed past me to get closer to the miracle man.

To me, though, Jimmy T looked like a dead ringer for that Indian guy in *Dances with Wolves*. You know, the one who calls out at the end, "Dances with Wolves, you will always be my friend."

Now, I know there are problems with that film. Like that it is yet another one of those *A Man Called Horse* movies where the white guy gets adopted and is even better at being an Indian than the real skins. Like that scene where he finds the buffalo herd before the Indians do? I mean, get real! Then there is, as Uncle Tommy told me, the fact that the dialogue coach was a Lakota woman. Uncle Tommy explained to me that there are two forms of Lakota, one masculine and one feminine. So that meant that every time Kevin Costner tried to speak Indian he was talking like a girl. But the one corny thought that went through my mind when I first saw Jimmy T, with his turquoise bracelets and that bone choker around

Joseph Bruchac

his neck, was that I wanted to hear him yell that to me: "Mitchell Sabattis, you will always be my friend." Like I said, corny.

But while everyone else made up to Jimmy T, I hung back.

That's always been my way. It seems to work for me, just as the few times when I do the opposite always seem to end up in disaster. Wait and See Sabattis, that's me. That's even the way I do it in sports. In basketball, I'm the guy who hangs back on the other team's fast break, so that when we get the ball again, I can take the pass way downcourt and lay it up. And in football, I'm the same. I follow my blockers when I'm at tailback, or when I'm playing D-back (I said we were big enough to have eleven-man football, but I didn't say we were big enough to not have half our players on both O and D) I hang off my man a little bit so that I can fool the quarterback into thinking he's not covered. When it comes to wild parties or doing crazy things with the guys, I'm the one who says, "Cool, but I'll catch you guys later." Plus I spend all the spare time I can over at Uncle Tommy's house, learning Indian stuff, and in the summers I work with him at the Indian Tourist Village. So even though I've got friends and a dual rep as a jock and a brainiac, I'm always close to being an outsider.

Which is how the three other new kids were being treated. Those White kids were getting the full-scale outsider treatment. I should explain, before you get the wrong idea, that their last name was a misnomer, because they weren't. They were black.

There had never been any black kids at our school before. It isn't that we're segregated. It is just that 99 percent of the African-American population in New York State live outside the northern Adirondack Mountain region. Black families pass through in tourist season. A few African Americans come to hunt and fish every year. They're treated just like any other flatlanders with money to add to the local economy. But as far as living here, Dr. Franklin White; his wife, Professor Efua Robinson White; their son, Randolph; and their twin daughters, Coretta and Rosa, were the first.

Dr. White, with his Ph.D. in Ecological Science, was the new director of the just-built Northern Adirondack Interpretive Center—NAIC for short. Dr. White's wife, who had been a full professor of American studies at Rutgers, was commuting to teach at Plattsburgh State, sixty miles away. They had bought the biggest and newest house in town, right on the point of the lake.

I knew all this because the week before school the Whites were the subject of a front-page article in our local paper, the *Long Pond Weekly Star*. The banner headline had read WELCOME THE WHITES and there had been a picture of all five of their smiling faces beneath it. It is a measure of our local journalism that no irony was intended.

(Interestingly enough, there hadn't been any article like that about Jimmy T's family, even though his dad had just been hired as NAIC's assistant director. The house they'd rented was on the other side of Long Pond and it wasn't lakefront.)

Randolph and his twin sisters were not smiling as they stood in the entrance to the school cafeteria. People nodded at them and said excuse me as they slipped by, but no one was making eye contact. No one was shaking their hands. Despite the fact that the three Whites were wearing clothes that were so top-of-the-line they might have been fashion models, everyone was avoiding looking at them. Maybe some of it was because no one quite knew what to say. All our images of African-American teenagers up here in the sticks are what we get on TV or in the movies. Rappers and gang-bangers predominate. So maybe our local Long Ponders were uncertain as to what the proper greeting would be. Like should it be "Yo, dog, whazzup?" or just a normal North Country "Hiya." Whichever, you could tell it was making Randolph and his sisters feel more and more like four-day-old roadkill.

It made me want to yell "For crying out loud! What's wrong with everyone!" Or maybe something else with a bunch of four-letter words in it. Uncle Tommy's had his influence on me, but I still let go with an old-fashioned profanity now and then.

I didn't, though. Instead I walked across the room, sort of in their direction, with my lunch tray in my hand. I was still hanging back, though, avoiding eye contact. I didn't really intend to get involved. I could see now that Randolph was shorter than me by a good four inches, but he probably outweighed me. You could tell there were muscles under his designer shirt. If it hadn't been for the fact that his jaw was clenched, you would have seen that his face was friendly and pleasant-looking. His sisters seemed shy, but easy on the eyes, too, the kind of girls who might make you look at least twice when they walked across a room. They were two years younger than their brother, but they were a lot taller—almost my height, and I'm six foot three. Although they were black, I realized that their skin color wasn't much darker than Uncle Tommy's.

Then, almost without realizing I was doing it, I did something that surprised myself. "Hey," I said, holding out my hand to Randolph.

He and his two sisters just about jumped. They'd been so

tense they hadn't even seen me come up to them. (Although I have been told that I have this way of sort of sneaking up on people without their noticing—"old Indian trick," as Uncle Tommy puts it.)

It only took Randolph half a second to recover his poise. "Hello," he said, cracking a small smile as he took my hand. That handshake was my first surprise. It wasn't a bone cruncher, like one jock gives another when they first meet. It was gentle, the way Indians shake hands with each other.

"I'm Mitch Sabattis. Welcome to Wrong Pond."

That made his smile a little broader. It's the oldest joke we have up here, but under the circumstances it had a little more zip than usual.

"I'm pleased to meet you," he said. No "yo." No "dog." Perfectly enunciated standard English. "I'm Randolph. These are my two younger sisters, Rosa and Coretta."

"Hello," they said, speaking and holding out their hands at the same time. Then, because they'd done it so perfectly in sync, almost like the start of a dance routine, they giggled.

I think it was a nervous giggle, which is probably why both Randolph and I laughed so hard then. Hard enough to make heads turn in our direction.

I'd managed to break the ice. The lunch table we took filled up, and before long other people were talking to the Whites. Not as many as hung around Jimmy T, but enough so that all I had to do now was mostly listen. It turned out I would probably be seeing a lot of Randolph, because he was as much into sports as me. He was a football player too. He'd played center at his old school. It wasn't the same school that Jimmy T had gone to, but they'd been in the same city league.

Joseph Bruchac

"Is he really a big-time QB?" Jacques Dennis asked.

"Yeah, he's as good as his clippings," Randolph said. The way he said it made me think there was something else he could have said about Jimmy T, but was holding back. I noticed, too, that the one time Jimmy T glanced over our way it seemed as if a dirty look passed between him and Randolph.

I didn't ask him about it. After all, we were just starting to get to know each other. I was looking forward to that, and his being a center made it even more likely we'd be spending time together. Even though Randolph had missed the preseason practice, I got the feeling he'd do just fine. He couldn't do any worse than Jacques, who was our current center. Everybody knew that Jacques actually hated the position. He just played it because there was nobody else as good as he was—which was pretty bad—at snapping the ball. What Jacques really loved was D-tackle, and we could use him there.

Rosa and Coretta were getting their share of attention too. Nancy Post, who loves clothes more than life itself, was chatting them up about accessorizing—whatever that means. Plus it turned out they were basketball players, and with their height they'd really add something to our girls' team, which had been depleted by the graduation of four senior starters.

After the conversation had gotten going real good around the table, I excused myself.

"Later," I said to Randolph.

"I'll look forward to that," he responded. I could tell he meant it.

I still hadn't had a chance to say hello to Jimmy T, and there seemed to be a little lull in the crowd around him where he was seated six tables down. But as soon as I walked over, Jimmy T stood up and turned his back on me. The "Hiya" I was about to speak died on my lips. He made his way quickly toward the door like he was late for an important appointment, even though the bell for classes wasn't going to ring for another five minutes. He clearly had something more important to do than talk to the local light-skinned breed. Most of the kids who'd been hanging on his every word followed along with him, although a couple of the guys who are on the team with me did turn back to give me a sympathetic shrug. But they still went with him.

Small as Long Pond High is, I didn't see Jimmy T for the rest of the school day. It was almost as if he was trying to avoid me, although for the life of me I couldn't figure out why. Sure, there were some mutterings about how there was bad blood between him and Randolph. They'd played on different teams that were bitter rivals. But I couldn't imagine that my being friendly with Randolph would keep him from looking me up. He must have heard I was Indian too.

Even if I did have a blond mother who could play the part of Brunhilde, I had always been the only kid in Long Pond School who really identified himself as Indian. Not that I was the only one with Indian ancestry. There's plenty of Native blood in the Adirondacks, but a lot of it is kept hidden. It was better in the past not to be Indian. And it's not that hard for people who are Indian to hide that fact—just keeping quiet and cutting your hair short and dressing like everybody else is usually enough. A lot of people with Indian blood do just that. Being Indian, even in the North Country, has always carried a lot of baggage in America. That was one of the reasons why I

Joseph Bruchac

hoped Jimmy T would make an effort to get to know me. I admired him for the fact that he wasn't hiding who he was. He wasn't afraid to let the world know he was a real Indian. Realer than me, a guy who had to dye his brown hair black to make it more Indian.

When I was little, I didn't think about it that much. My dad, who was as Indian-looking as Cochise, could always handle it with his good nature. People who started out hostile would end up buying him beers. Usually a few too many. They were surprised at how he could hold his booze, what with all they say about Indians not being able to drink without getting all crazy. I don't think my dad was even that drunk the night he died. After all, it was the tractor-trailer that skidded on the ice, then veered into the wrong lane and hit my dad's pickup, not the other way around.

I started hanging out with Uncle Tommy after my mother and I got back from Sweden. Getting to know him, even though he wasn't really a relative, was like getting to know things about my dad that I'd never known before.

I remember the only time Uncle Tommy ever asked me why I was hanging around him so much.

"My dad," I said, "never taught me how to be an Indian."

"Mitchell," Uncle Tommy said to me, "white men taught us how to be Indians. Before that, we were just people."

"Hey, Chief," Jacques Dennis said to me as I closed my locker.

"Hey," I said. "What's up."

"It's all good," Jacques said. He was beaming. "Randolph

is cool. A real center, hey? Yes!" He held up his right hand and I high-fived him, wondering as I did so if Randolph ever high-fived or if he simply insisted on a gentlemanly handshake.

Practice was without pads. We'd get them next week; for now it was just running and a few easy drills. Coach Carson pulled Randolph aside, though, along with Bun Bowman, who was trying to take over the QB spot this year. After ten minutes of watching them do snaps together, Coach nodded his head and called for me. My other job on the team for the last two years has been to be the kicker. I paced it off and then yelled, "Hike." The most perfect spiral long snap I'd ever seen came whizzing back at me like a bullet.

"All right!" Coach Carson yelled, raising both fists. It surprised both him and the rest of the team, since Coach has always been a man who doesn't show his feelings. But I had to admit I understood. Maybe I wouldn't end up chasing balls snapped four feet over my head or six feet to my left this season. Jacques Dennis simply sucked as a long snapper.

Coach Carson folded his arms and regained his composure. "Again," he said.

And Randolph did it again . . . and again . . . and again. Every snap was picture-perfect.

Then Jimmy T showed up. Late as he was, and despite the fact he'd missed the wind sprints, Coach Carson welcomed him. Before long it was obvious that he could throw not just long balls and bullets, but also touch passes.

I didn't catch any. Coach Carson kept me working with Randolph, getting our rhythm down. After a while he had Bun join us to take snaps so I could try some point-after attempts.

Joseph Bruchac

My year in Sweden, when I would have been in eighth grade, I played soccer as a striker. So I'm the best place kicker on our team. With Jacques's erratic snaps, Coach hadn't dared try kicking the PAT all last season. Whatever extra points we made were on runs or passes.

For the rest of practice, Coach Carson walked around alternately humming a tune that sounded suspiciously like "Happy Days Are Here Again" and then catching himself at it and clamming up. But, despite how hard he tried to control himself, he was feeling good. This was the year that he had it all. This was finally the season when his Long Pond Lumberjacks were going to win the division.

I wasn't completely convinced. Maybe no one else had seen it, but I could still sense the tension building between Jimmy T and Randolph. The last half hour of practice, Jimmy T was taking snaps from him. They were both so good that they got into a real rhythm after a while. That's the key, you know, that rhythm a center and a quarterback need to make everything come out right. I could tell that they both loved what they were doing so much that they'd forgotten, for the moment at least, whatever bad blood was between them in the past. What worried me, though, was what would occur after practice.

But nothing bad happened. They just went to lockers at opposite ends of the room and ignored each other. In fact, after we hit the showers, Jimmy T, toweling off his long hair, finally said something to me, even though it was in a guarded voice.

"Nice job, kicker."

"Thanks," I replied.

It made me feel great to get that praise. For a half a second

I wondered if maybe I should try to start a real conversation with him now. But I left it at that. It was better to hang back. No point in pushing my luck.

The fourth week of school, I got invited over to Randolph's house to meet his mom and dad. By then we'd already had our first two games, and won them both. I hadn't caught any passes yet, but I'd kicked eleven extra points and two field goals, which gives you an idea of just how well the Long Pond Lumberjacks were doing with Jimmy T as our quarterback and Randolph as our center. Whatever there was between them, they seemed to put it aside as soon as the whistle blew and we ran onto the field. They just concentrated on the game.

I saw right off how important concentrating on the game was for Jimmy T. His father was a Yeller. There're different kinds of parents that come to high school football games. Some are always cheering for their kids. Even when they do something dumb, those parents call out things like "You vill do it next time, Mitchell." Yeah, my mom is that kind of parent. Others just sit in the stands and watch politely and cheer when everyone else does, not doing anything to call attention to themselves or embarrass their kid. That was how Randolph's mom and dad always behaved. Then there are the Yellers. They don't stay in the stands—they walk up and down as close to the field as they can get. They scream at the referees, at the coaches, at the players on the other team.

Mr. Black was the worst Yeller I'd ever seen. He was tall and raven-haired, like Jimmy. But he didn't wear his hair long or have on any Indian jewelry. I guessed that was because he

Joseph Bruchac

didn't want to call attention to himself at his job. But he surely called attention to himself during those first two games.

Jimmy hardly made a mistake. But the few times he did, Mr. Black was bellowing at his son louder than Coach Carson. He yelled so much that his face got beet red.

"Can't you take a snap?" he shouted, throwing his hat on the ground. "For Christ's sake, Jimmy, didn't you see that open man? Wake up, Ref, Number Eighty-nine was offsides. You're brain-dead, Ref, brain-dead! Hey, Number Fifty-eight, you stink. Come on, Jimmy. You're playing like you're asleep, you damn loser."

Jimmy tried to ignore it. He just kept playing. But I noticed how flushed his face got when his father called him a loser. At one point in our second game, Coach even went over to Mr. Black and asked him to tone it down some because the refs were ready to call a penalty on our team.

By now I was spending a lot of my time with Randolph. He was in advanced classes (at least as advanced as it is possible for any class to be in Wrong Pond High) with me, so we saw each other all the time. That was a change for me. I've always had lot of acquaintances in school. You know the kind—you pass each other in the hall, give each other the high sign.

But I'd never had any real friends my age. Randolph was getting to be one.

Jimmy T, on the other hand, I hardly even saw—unless it was his back going the other way. He wasn't in one single class with me. It seemed he had some academic troubles. He was passing things, but just barely. His grades were just high enough to keep him eligible for football.

"If it hadn't been for his father putting pressure on the

Guidance Department," somebody said as Jimmy T made his way down the crowded hallway, "Geronimo there would have been stuck in vocational classes."

I don't think Jimmy T heard that remark, but I did. It was the kind of thing some kids who can't play sports say about athletes, but it troubled me. It made me wish I could find the courage to really talk with Jimmy. It seemed to me that maybe he was doing what a lot of Indian kids do, not living up to his potential because he didn't want to play by *their* rules. But Jimmy still avoided me whenever he could, and I didn't make it a point to seek him out.

That evening I spent with Randolph's family went even better than I'd expected, even though I got the shock of my life. The Whites were nice, everything you'd want a dad and mom to be. They were interested in their kids, but they didn't pry. They had clear rules, but they trusted their kids to follow them. The big surprise came when we were at the dinner table and Mrs. White turned to me.

"Do you speak any Abenaki, Mitchell?" she said.

I hadn't expected that, but the little smile Randolph gave me told me he had.

"Some," I said. "My mom's not Indian, but she's been encouraging me to learn more."

"That's very good," Mr. White said. His voice was one of those deep ones that kind of reverberate in your chest. "I've always been a race man myself. Young people should be proud of their history, proud of their race."

"Plural, dear," Mrs. Randolph said. "Races."

Across the table from me, Randolph looked like he was so amused that he was about to bust a gut, while Coretta and

Rosa were smiling at each other in that way twins have of showing they are thinking exactly the same thing.

"Randolph," Mr. White said, "greet your friend in the language of your great-grandparents."

"Osi yo ogi na li i," Randolph said in a voice I'd never heard him use before. He wasn't laughing as he said it. Whatever it was, I could tell that he really meant what he said. My mouth, though, couldn't catch up to my mind.

"Huh?" was all I could say in return.

"That is 'Hello, my friend,' in Tsalagi, the Cherokee language," Mrs. White said.

It turned out that both Mr. White and his wife had not just Cherokee, but also Choctaw ancestors. His great-great-grandparents had gone on the Trail of Tears to Oklahoma, where the name White Path had been shortened to White. They had kept the Cherokee language in their family the way some folks keep a family Bible.

"Cherokee hair," Mrs. White said, reaching out to stroke the heads of her two daughters.

"Most African Americans," Mr. White said, "have at least some Indian ancestry, as I expect you know already, Mitchell. But I'm afraid most white Americans are not about to accept that fact."

Even though Randolph was clicking as Jimmy T's center, there was that unspoken tension between them. I know now what it was, and it wasn't their fault. But the day it came to a head almost spelled the ruin of our whole football season. We were in practice. Coach Carson had just gotten an emergency call and had gone into the school to answer it. We were on our own.

I don't know what started it. But I heard Jimmy T say the "n" word. It shocked me so much that I turned around to see him staring at Randolph. Randolph was looking back at him like he couldn't believe what he'd heard.

Then Randolph shook his head. "Better than being a faker, pal."

Jimmy T threw the football he was holding—hard, and right at Randolph. The football made a loud thump like a drumstick hitting a big drum as it bounced off Randolph's broad, thick-muscled chest and flew right back into Jimmy T's face. Blood spurted out of Jimmy T's nose. He lunged toward Randolph, who still stood there without moving. He looked as calm and solid as an oak tree, but I could tell how angry he was, angry enough to tear Jimmy T apart. So, quick as Jimmy T moved, I was quicker. I got in between the two of them and wrapped my arms around Jimmy, pinning his arms to his sides. Blood was still pumping out of his nose and his olive face was flushed with rage. His eyes were almost popping out of his head. He was so furious that he couldn't talk.

"Jimmy," I hissed into his ear, pressing my cheek hard against his and getting my own face smeared with his blood, "Stop it, man. You are better than this."

I felt the tension go out of him as I said that. I slowly let go and stepped back. Jimmy T was looking into my face, really looking at me for the first time. His eyes were filled with tears.

"No I'm not," he whispered back. Then he turned and ran toward the school, holding the small towel that he had hung on his waist up to his bloody nose. I followed him for a few steps, then decided it was better to leave him alone and check

Joseph Bruchac

on Randolph, who was still rooted to that same spot.

"It's okay," Randolph said as I walked up to him. "I don't blame him. I blame his father."

There was no time to find out what he meant just then, because Coach Carson came back and I had to explain how Jimmy T had accidentally gotten hit in the nose by the ball and had gone in to stop the bleeding and get cleaned up.

Jimmy T didn't come back out on the field that day. In the locker room, when we were alone, Randolph explained what he meant.

"His father hates my dad," Randolph said, tying his shoes hard. "He thinks that *he* should have been the director of the center. People have heard him say that the only reason my father got the position was because of his race." Randolph shook his head. "My dad won't talk about it, but my mom said that the two of them were friends in graduate school; people used to joke about it being all Black and White back then. But then my father started doing better than him. Now it's as if they're enemies who have to work together every day. It's pretty sad."

"So it's cool with Jimmy T now?" I said. I was amazed at how calm Randolph was about it all.

"It's cool," Randolph said.

And it turned out that it was. Jimmy T was in school and at practice the next day like nothing had happened. He didn't apologize to Randolph and they didn't shake hands. But they did keep working together, trusting each other on the field the way a good center and quarterback have to trust each other. And we kept winning football games.

The next shocker came one day when I was filling up my

truck at our one local gas station. It was the old beater Chevy truck I'd bought with some of the money I'd earned working summers at the Indian Village, which is part of our local "Wild West" tourist attraction where Uncle Tommy has worked for years. Because of that year in Sweden, I got held back a grade when I returned to the U.S.A., so even though I was only a junior, I was plenty old enough to have a real driver's license and not just a learner's permit. Anyhow, who should pull up to the other pump but Jimmy T's mother.

I didn't know who she was right away. I'd never seen Mrs. Black at games. She really kept to herself and didn't go out much. The rumor was that she was sick, but I had found myself wondering after our first few games if she didn't want to be around when her husband was stalking the sidelines and yelling things at their son. So it surprised me when this puffy-cheeked woman wearing dark eye shadow got out of her car and came up to me.

"Are you Mitchell Sabattis?" she said. "You must be, aren't you?"

"Yes, ma'am," I said, not quite sure what this was all about.

"I'm Iris Black, Jimmy's mother."

She was so close to me that I could smell the alcohol on her breath. Her eyes were real bright. My dad's eyes used to get bright like that after he'd had his first few beers.

"Pleased to meet you, Mrs. Black," I said.

She grabbed me so hard by the wrist that I almost dropped the gas cap I was starting to screw back on.

"You have been so good to my son. He just talks about you all the time. You just do not know how important you are to him. He wishes he could be like you."

Then Mrs. Black leaned over, kissed me on my cheek, turned back around, got into her car, and drove off without even getting gas.

Those surprises got me thinking. And when I really start thinking, some of the things that Uncle Tommy's told me come into my mind. One of them was that you never can tell what is in another person's heart by the way they look on the outside.

What was really in Jimmy T's heart?

I found out the Saturday after I met Jimmy T's mom. It was the Big Creek game. We were down 13 to zip. The Long Pond Lumberjacks had turned back into the Wrong Pond Flapjacks. Everything Jimmy had done in the first half, it was like he was moving in slow motion. He couldn't complete a pass; hell, he was barely even able to make a clean handoff.

Like always, Jimmy's dad was on the sidelines, yelling. But this time he wasn't yelling at the referees or the other players. His whole attention was on Jimmy. He'd been critical of Jimmy when we'd been winning. Now that we were behind, he was just plain brutal.

"You're a loser, kid, a damn loser," he bellowed like a wounded moose. "I always knew it. You're the same as your damn mother."

Just about the whole team was following Jimmy's lead. If it hadn't been for a few good plays on D, we would have been down by twice that score. It was the worst first half of football I've ever been part of. Finally, and none too soon, it was halftime.

Jimmy sat with his head down in the locker room. No one was talking to him—not even Coach Carson. We had to be back on the field in five minutes. Coach motioned to the team.

"Let's go," he said. Jimmy didn't move.

Coach grabbed my arm before I could get out the door. "Mitch," he whispered. "You're the only player with his head still in this game. Talk to him."

"Why me?" I said.

Coach looked up toward the sky in exasperation. "Jeezum, do you always have to go back and forth between being brilliant and brain-dead, Sabattis? Just do it."

From behind Coach's back, Randolph held up his hand and gave me the thumbs-up sign. He believed in me too, even if I didn't.

Coach Carson shut the locker room door and I went over to sit across from Jimmy T.

"I never really said I was Indian," Jimmy T said without looking up. "We moved around so much. And whenever I showed up at a new school wearing this jewelry and with all this hair, people assumed I was Native American. It was so much easier that I just went along with it. It was like I was somebody better, you know? But it's like White said: I'm a phony. My real middle name is Tomas, not Thorpe. There's not a drop of Indian blood in our family. We're Hungarian, for Christ's sake."

He slammed his fist against a locker. I didn't say anything.

"God," Jimmy T said. "I'm nothing. My dad is right." He looked across at me, and I could see the pain in his eyes. "There's no way I can ever live up to his standards. You know what he told me before the game? He said it didn't matter how many football games I won, I was still a born loser. I'll never do anything right."

Joseph Bruchac

I kept my mouth shut. That was another lesson Uncle Tommy taught me: Never interrupt people when they start speaking from their heart.

Jimmy T took another deep breath. He leaned forward and pulled at his long hair. "I wish I really was Indian. I'm not real like you, Mitchell." He clenched his fists and looked down at his feet. "It was just so much easier pretending to be somebody, just to hide."

"I know that," I said.

Maybe somewhere deep inside I'd always understood why Jimmy T had avoided me. It wasn't because I wasn't real enough. It was because he'd been afraid I'd see that he was playing a part. He'd been a pretend Indian to get away from the pain in his real life. But I didn't hate him for it. All the real Indians I've known have done their share of trying to get away from the pain too. Or at least they've known that pain. Like Uncle Tommy told me, pain is part of the admission fee for being human.

In that moment, I knew that we'd have our undefeated football season. Of course, I'm writing this after all that happened, so it's easy for me to say now. But, trust me, I did. I knew we'd go back out on the field with our hearts in the game. Maybe I didn't foresee my snagging that interception for a TD, but you can't know everything.

But as Jimmy T sat there across from me in the locker room with the look of a lost soul on his face, the thing I knew most strongly was that there was only one thing I could say.

"I've got this friend named Uncle Tommy Fox. He's taught me a lot of things over the years. When he comes back, I'm going to introduce you to him. But for right now, let me just tell you what I know *he'd* tell you."

I paused and waited until Jimmy T lifted his head up again to look at me.

"What?" Jimmy T said, looking like a drowning person who hopes someone will throw him a life preserver. "What would he say?"

I could hear Uncle Tommy's voice. He was talking not just to Jimmy T but to me as well, sharing a lesson both of us needed to learn.

"Whoever you are is real enough. Underneath our skins, everyone's blood is red."

by Sherri Winston

Here it comes. No matter how many times I watch the video, it gets me when her voice falters and breaks:

"I've had my hair pulled, my stomach punched, my property—my books and such—destroyed. I report it, but reporting a problem here at Grays doesn't mean fixing the problem. Not if you're Haitian. Some of the black Americans here think all Haitians are stupid boat people. They make fun of us and hurt us."

Emmaline is on-screen, her face larger than life, commanding the attention of all of us in the room. I'm the one asking the questions—off-screen. What do she and other Haitian students want from our high school? She answers, "Haitian students want to be treated equal. Right now, that's not how we're treated. We come to school afraid because we do not feel safe. We don't have someone on our side. Not Anyone."

Grains of light separate inside the room like the gray pixels of a digital photo. He is watching me through the grayness.

Anyone. Anyone is glaring, seething . . . and listening. He may be able to ignore Emmaline and the others when no other grown-ups are watching, but today, we have company. Today, Anyone is definitely paying attention.

Channel 5 news anchor Courtney Basil breezes toward me in a cool, fuzzy cloud of Chanel No. 5, my mother's favorite. "That was brilliant. Brilliant," she repeats over and over. Muckety-mucks from the school board nod and bob their heads. Anyone, aka Principal Malcolm Avery King, locks eyes with me. Instinctively I reach for the spot on my arm, rub the skin. A few months ago, when I was in here with him, he snatched my arm so hard he almost pulled it loose. I had dared to question the treatment of Haitian students. He doesn't like being questioned. My arm hurt for days. His smile is so beautiful I almost wince. I exhale to stop my trembling. But I refuse to look away. Screw him.

"Noelle, when we decided to launch an at-large reporting project using high school students to tell real stories, our expectations were high, but we had no idea anyone would produce a piece as insightful and important as what you have screened for us today," exclaims Courtney Basil. She says:

"Of course, with Christmas only a little over a week away, I think it'd be best to go with your homeless story first. We'll save the hard-hitting Haitian story for after the holidays. Great job!"

Sherri Winston

Langston and Antonia cling to the doorjamb. Class president and student council president, respectively. They are afraid. They know that the news footage we screened earlier with King was different from what we just saw.

"We've got to go to class," Antonia says. Langston steps on the back of her shoe, the two of them are so desperate to leave.

"Principal King, I want to thank you again for allowing us to select your school and your student to participate in our pilot project," says Travis Hall, news producer.

"Noelle is one of our finest students, no question. It has been our extreme pleasure to work with you and open our school to your news station," King says, extending his hand and flashing his brilliant smile. I cannot control the shudder. "Goodness knows her revelations have given me much to consider."

Courtney Basil squeezes my shoulder and Travis Hall says, "We have to get back. Strange weather front moving in. When we left, the meteorologists were on the rooftop. Meteorologists. Weird bunch."

Lights buzz. Sepia hands trip thickly across the face of a clock carved in the shape of Africa. When the door has closed, King's smile, gleaming though it has been, evaporates like mist in the rain forest. Now we are lion and prey on an

African savannah. I edge away, partly glad the smile has gone. I hate his smile. He smiles like he can't see you.

He smiles like my father.

The clock's hands urge time forward.

And the lion moves closer to his prey.

"Miss Truth, please have a seat."

Once I am seated, he positions himself, arms folded across his body, head back just enough to ensure that no portion of the Dr. Martin Luther King Jr. oil painting is obscured. He looks as if he's posing to be immortalized on a postage stamp. His tenure at Grays High School has been filled with poses.

"I'll say this for you, kid, you're one heck of a journalist." The smile returns.

"Principal King—"

He cuts me off with a mere flick of his wrist, "Please, Miss Truth, allow me to finish. Now, the piece you did on the students pulling together to feed and clothe homeless and needy kids, that was fabulous and definitely exhibits the proud spirit and reputation that all of us see as a hallmark of Grays. . . ."

However.

Principal King arrived at Paul Grays High School in October of my freshman year. Our school had been troubled with conflicts between African-American and white students for decades. As the black population in the school grew and the white population became poorer, the school's climate got even

Sherri Winston

worse, and Grays and the school board took a lot of heat.

Then along came the principal with the great suits and the great smile. Racial unrest between black and white students began to vanish. King takes credit. Of course, the fact that so many white families moved away doesn't seem to matter to King.

But point to a problem, something he hasn't fixed, and he'll hurt you. My sophomore year, a senior here, Darren Betters—real popular, excellent student—recognized some of King's tactics as underhanded. He saw how King allowed African-American students to get privileges that Caribbean blacks, not to mention white or Hispanic students, couldn't get. Darren called him on it. Next thing anybody knew, Darren went from being senior class president to being suspended. He was mysteriously kept out of the yearbook, and rumor has it King even tried to interfere with his acceptance at Duke.

Then my junior year, I challenged King. Told him too many non-African-American students were treated like second-class citizens. We were right here, in this office. He yanked me from my seat and told me to get out and go cool off. Fifteen minutes later, I was on a ladder helping the student council hang signs for an upcoming blood drive. I never saw King come up behind me, but when the ladder shook, I tumbled from the top rung to the floor with my arm—the same one he'd grabbed—twisted beneath me. I wound up with a nasty sprain and the kind of experience you don't exactly write about in the yearbook.

He swore it was an accident.

He is pacing now.

"Your Haitian story, Noelle, concerns me."

"That's good. One of the first rules of good journalism is to challenge your audience. I'm glad I was able to do that."

He stops pacing. We're back on the savannah again, lion and prey.

"Let me spell it out for you, No-elle," he says, arms planted on either side of my chair. "Grays students are my family, my children, and I take care of my own. When I got here morale was low, test scores were low, and the general attitude of African-American students was just plain terrible. I came in and made these kids feel like somebody. Made them—"

"You're too close to me, Mr. King. Please step away." Eye to eye, that's how we are. He looks shocked by my tone, but he doesn't move.

"Mr. King," I sit up higher in the chair. "Please. Back. Away."

He takes a step back. Then he is on me, yanking me from the chair to within an inch of his face. "Little girl," he says, "do you think I'm playing some kind of game with you?"

For a second, my eyes squeeze shut. Emmaline's words, the words of dozens of Haitian kids I interviewed while putting that news piece together, return. They said they wanted to feel

safe. No. Even better. Protected. Like somebody, anybody—
Anyone—had their back.

"Are you playing with me, Noelle? Switching the video like
that. Showing me one thing when it's just us at the school, but
waiting till we've got company to spring your little surprise.
Was that supposed to scare me?"

I want to feel big and powerful. I want to tell him to kiss
my black behind. Or to say it politically: Kiss my African-
American booty.

But I'm scared, so I keep quiet.

He pulls away, but just an inch or two, a slight smile
returning to his face. "Noelle, sweetheart, you're going to be
gone next fall. Probably to a good school. You don't want to
jeopardize that, right?"

More nonverbal communication from me. Is this how he
threatened Darren Betters?

"So why risk your future over what we might as well call
an unfortunate series of misunderstandings. Perhaps your
American black classmates have been insensitive to the plight
of their island classmates, but that's our business. Grays' business. We don't need to broadcast that. I'm sure they were just
blowing off steam. I'm sure they didn't mean any harm."

"Funny," I say, forcing my hand to still itself, my feet to
remain flat rather than rat-a-tat tapping. "I'll bet that's what that
white principal used to say when those redneck cracker kids
were kicking the crap out of the black kids for all those years."

The lion's eyes go wild. "Now listen up, you snotty little
traitor. This stops right here, right now. You might think you're
clever, pulling that stunt, screening your little interviews in
front of outsiders. Well, guess what? It doesn't matter. You run

that tape of those dumb-ass Haitians bellyaching about how they're treated at my school and I swear to God, there'll be snow in Miami before you know any peace."

The King has spoken.

He snatches me to my feet.

"Don't even bother trying to report this to anyone, because you'll come off sounding insane. People love me around here. And considering how things are at home for you right now with your mom . . ."

My eyes burn into him. For a moment, his dark pupils become video screens and Emmaline and her pain flash across the bridge of his nose. The time I spent working on that story, interviewing Emmaline and all the others, carrying their pain around in my notebook, gave me a companion. They talked about feeling scared and unsafe. I feel scared and unsafe all the time.

All the time.

Used to be I looked at my dad like he was some kind of superhero.

Now I know better.

Now I know he can't protect me from anything. Or Anyone.

"Leave my mother out of it," I say, sliding under the tent he has made with his body. When I look back, he has straightened. His smile is beatific. He gives a mock shudder as I throw open the door, almost slamming into his secretary.

"Again, Miss Truth, congratulations on your excellent work, and remember, it never snows in Miami."

Sherri Winston

At the hospital two days later, Mommy and I lie to each other, as we have been doing for several months now.

I ask: "How're you doing today?"

She says: "I'm feeling stronger."

She asks: "How're things at school? How's your news project?"

And I say: "Fine."

I toss another blanket on her feet. The room is ice-cold. Chemotherapy. After five years of remission, the breast cancer returned. She will not make it this time. We do not acknowledge that. We also don't discuss my father. Coach Deion Truth, former running back, former NFL all-star. My dad. In a lot of ways, he's been gone since Mom's cancer the first time around. She never complained or cried, not in front of me, but Daddy, he spent ten months looking like she was already dead. He was scared to death. So he hid from us.

Even though the cancer treatments appeared to work, me and Mommy both saw how he threw himself into his career. Retired from his team, became hungry to find an assistant coaching gig, something, anything that would keep him on the road and on the go . . . away.

"I got you a birthday present," she whispers, eyes half open. She has no eyebrows, and where she once had long, lush ebony braids, a red silk scarf covers tufts of hair the medicine hasn't burned from her scalp.

"Mommy, my birthday isn't for a few more days. I thought I told you I didn't need anything."

Every word hurts. Paper-cut incisions against the soft, pink meat of my heart. I'm a Christmas baby. Always wants me to know she's celebrating my birthday and Christmas.

She loves me so much I can't look at her sometimes. Even

before the cancer, I sometimes was afraid to love her back.

Crinkling, shimmering oyster pink paper embossed with foil gold trumpets falls off the box. I'm home with my gift. Mommy was too tired. I didn't want to wear her down.

I remove a framed photograph. The frame is new. I recognize it from the hospital gift shop. Picturing her shuffling around to buy me a gift makes me smile, and I break out in a sweat.

Damn! It's not fair. I'd give anything not to be me right now.

Then I look at the photo. It's me when I was . . . five? I'm under the tree, wrapped in gift paper.

She must have had it retouched, enlarged. Her reflection in one of the glass balls on the Christmas tree shows clearly. Her smile almost matches mine. It was just the two of us at home alone that Christmas. As usual.

At least, that's what I thought. I look closer and see what I've never before noticed. Hands. Big and strong and in the background. Hands guiding me to safety, protecting me. Then, in a fuzzy sort of way, I remember wrapping myself in paper and falling beneath the tree. Almost falling. A pair of hands caught me, held me.

My father's hands.

Langston stops me in the hallway.

"You know he'll go ape if you let them show that tape," he whispers. Langston is senior class president. It is rumored King tampered with the vote tabulations because he knew Langston

Sherri Winston

would be easier to control than the fiery Sean Pierre-Pierre.

It's just a rumor. Florida politics. Anything is possible.

"He has no say over content. That was the agreement. Period." I slam my locker and we walk toward the parking lot together in silence. An orange slice cuts across the sky and a frosty gust makes us both shudder.

"Man, it's freezing out here," Langston says. He's bouncing around. The sky is flat and white and the air feels cold and wet.

"Brrr . . . Maybe we'll hear on the news tonight that hell is freezing over," I say as I climb into my car.

He's laughing over his shoulder as he jogs away, and I hear him yell, "Nope, hell can't be freezing over 'cause I haven't gotten laid yet. And that's truly the first sign."

I can't resist. I drive alongside his car before he can pull away. "No, Lang, that's the first sign of the Apocalypse!"

It's harmless flirting. Langston is sort of cute, the guy I will no doubt remember ten years from now and ask myself, "Why didn't we . . . ?"

I want to hold on to such thoughts a while longer, but as soon as my car hits Broward Boulevard my thoughts shift from Langston to my father. I'm gripping the steering wheel way too tight.

Daddy. He called last night sounding all concerned on the answering machine. I heard him leave a message. I didn't even pick up. They have phones at the hospital. If he really wants to know how Mommy is doing, let him go to the source.

At school, I've managed to avoid King Anyone, despite his clumsy attempts to intimidate me with his King of the Jungle glare.

Mommy looks up from her bed. The red headscarf has been replaced with a vibrant purple paisley. I am poised to reach for her when suddenly the smile greets me.

The beautiful smile. Principal King is at her bedside, holding her hand.

"Noelle!" His voice is slow, heavy. Inside my book bag my most dangerous weapon is a dull No. 2 pencil, inadequate for slaying the Antichrist.

"Baby, I'm glad you're here." Mommy sits up, or at least tries.

"Daddy called last night," she says. "He thinks he might make it in for a visit today. Says he tried to reach you at home, but he got the machine." Now her eyes have locked with mine. She knows I was ignoring my father.

"Come on in, Noelle. I was just talking with your mother about our 'situation.' You know, what we discussed about the Haitian students?" He grins broadly.

He has shared his version with my mother. He has told her that while he applauds my initiative for bringing to light issues of which he was not aware, he fears that if I air the Haitian story I will place not only the featured students at risk, but perhaps myself as well.

"Your principal thinks some of the Haitian students might belong to gangs. Thinks you might be in danger. Is that a possibility?"

Her voice quivers. She isn't strong enough for this. I spoke with the doctor yesterday. It's not going well. She is breaking down, one system at a time.

What choice do I have?

"Mommy, I had no idea Principal King felt so strongly about my piece," I say sweetly.

Sherri Winston

Now I'm smiling, and because we once shared the same smile, mother and daughter, I know it is my most radiant, get-a-second-helping-of-dessert smile.

I squeeze her toes, then massage the soles of her feet. She wiggles her toes. We lock eyes again, Mommy and me.

Of course, she knows I'm lying.

"I love you, baby," she says. Then she closes her eyes.

I look directly at the grinning, shining Principal King and I say brightly, "You can trust that you will get just what you deserve for coming here today."

"How long has it been? How long? HOW LONG? Somebody get me research on the phone!" She's shouting, the beautiful Courtney Basil. She and the producer appear flushed. Chaos. It is Christmas Eve. Weather will lead the five o'clock news and Courtney is anchor. My news assistant is Kara. She helped me edit both my Haitian piece and the piece on getting clothes for homeless teens. The homeless clothes story is supposed to run now; they plan to "save" the Haitian story.

But that's not what I told the young college intern guy over at the other desk where they queue up the tapes.

We won't be hearing about selfless students who help homeless teens. Not today.

My heart has jammed against my rib cage. If I close my eyes, I see my mother's face as I sat with her last night. My father never showed. Like all the best jerks, he sent lovely flowers. My fists are knotted against my thighs. My big moment has come. I will defeat evil. Power to the little people. No more fear.

It unfolds as languidly as a sunset over one of Haiti's touristy beaches.

The newscast begins, and weather is the big story. Live footage from the malls, and ha, ha, ha, and ho, ho, ho, a check-in with Santa.

Everybody feels good on Christmas Eve. Some traffic, local news, travel news, then the second half hour. Courtney Basil beams as she says, "Noelle Truth continues our high school correspondents' series with . . ."

And then, Emmaline's voice crackles in the newsroom.

When it is done, I cannot breathe. "Nice job, kid. Welcome to the newsroom." A stranger pats me on the back. A meteorologist wearing a Santa hat and elf house shoes dashes over, practically screaming about air vectors and troughs going through Miami.

Kara glances at me, looking bewildered. Courtney remains at the news desk, but her face shows confusion. My head feels the way it does sometimes when I inhale too many fumes at the gas station.

Cold rain falls in stubborn droplets and the wind whips against the white twinkle lights entwined around the trunks of palm trees. Emmaline's grateful voice is in my ear, saying, "At least you did something. You should be proud."

I *want* to feel proud of what I've done, but I cannot. Emmaline and I have been friends for years. Black kids who pick on her for being Haitian make me sick. I wanted to do something to make her understand, if for only a few seconds, that someone was listening. Maybe make her feel safe. Making King look foolish was a bonus.

My mother will not live to see another Christmas. Not without a miracle. Defeating Principal King a thousand times cannot change that fact. I wanted to be a champion for the Haitian students because I don't know how to champion my own cause. How do you save your mother from cancer and your father from running away?

I flip my cell phone shut. I'm walking behind the news station when I hear the slurp of tires.

"Stupid, stupid girl! You're as stupid as the Haitians! You might as well be one of them." King has lurched from his car and is chasing me. Ranting about how he'll ruin me and how he's in control at Grays High School and nobody's gonna stick their nose in his business.

He is shrieking at me, lunging, slipping. I wrench my back trying to keep away. Out of the corner of my eye, I spot Kara. She and a cameraman must have been heading for one of the news vans.

My face is wet. Soft, wet, cool—what? Snow. Fat, wet flakes of snow. I haven't seen snow since we lived in Baltimore. Even King pauses to take in the frozen spectacle. Then he grabs me again. His hands close on my throat. I slip on the ice and we both fall. Hard. Sharp light pierces my eyes, and I wince. The glare from his smile?

It takes a while for either of us to realize the camera has been rolling and that Kara is trying to wrest me free of his grip.

By eleven o'clock, I had gone from journalist, to subject of the news. As I sat in the studio, my knees knocking together beneath the desk, I wondered how King was doing in the Broward County jail.

The beautiful Courtney smiled radiantly at her unseen audience and announced, "For the first time in almost forty years, Miami has been blanketed with snow."

Now, as I lie awake at the foot of Mommy's bed, feeling my scalp massaged by unseen fingers, I do not rush to open my eyes. Christmas morning. I was on the Today show.

I stretch and blink. Pale blues and soft shades of gray and yellow fleck across my eyes. I am surprised to find that the fingers massaging my scalp are not Mommy's.

"Daddy?"

"It's a miracle," he says softly.

I stiffen, glance over, see Mommy asleep beside me, so frail she looks like a breathing silhouette. I glance back at him and he nods toward the window.

"The snow. Bad weather kept me from making my flight."

He smiles, a beautiful, hopeful smile. Then it breaks apart.

"I . . . That man, that principal. He could have hurt you. I—"

His voice cracks. My head is still swimming from yesterday, so I'm trying to keep the drama to a minimum.

"I'm fine, Daddy," I say, rising to my elbow, aware that

his hand has dropped to my arm and he is clinging to me—protectively. I don't want him to let go. When I start to get up, he squeezes my elbow, holds me in place.

"When I saw your story . . ." His voice breaks again. He looks embarrassed, like maybe he didn't even realize I was into journalism. "You did an excellent job. Maybe now someone will pay those students some attention. Maybe someone will be there when they need them."

Silence piles on top of us. I look away, and he grabs my fingers. Mom stirs, and I'm struggling to swallow my tears.

"They deserve to feel safe, Daddy."

He nods. Mom stirs, a silhouette in motion. She is still sleeping. He whispers, "Everyone deserves to feel safe." He tucks me under his arm and I drift back asleep, watching the crystal-clear drip of medicine run through the tube and into my mother's arm, while outside snowy Afros crest the tops of the nearby palm trees.

Snow

THE HEARTBEAT OF THE Soul OF THE WORLD

by René Saldaña Jr.

On the day of PD's funeral, the sun beat down on the crowd gathered at the cemetery. A good many of us from the barrio were there. A few from the high school marching band were also in attendance. The heat made us all slouch, sweaty and heavy.

PD's family took up the two rows of chairs directly in front of the coffin, the lid closed for the sake of PD's mother. She had cried and cried when she heard her boy was dead. Just another night out with friends, on his way home, the officer told her. He'd got in a wreck. The other driver'd been drinking. Somehow PD's right arm had been cut off cleanly just below the elbow. His face and head misshapen but without a bruise or scratch. This last part the cop didn't tell her. She saw for herself at the morgue.

That night, a few hours after news of the wreck, one of the boys in Peñitas, hiding from his parents on the roof of his house, nearly fell from his perch when he heard PD's mom screaming out her dead son's name: "Ay, mi Pedro, mi Pedrito. Ay, Diosito Santo. Porqué, Diosito?" The boy thought it was La

Llorona crying out for her drowned babies, and that's when he almost fell.

Today at the funeral, PD's mom was all cried out. All she did was grab at her chest and moan, wrinkle her face, moan some more. Times like these—the heat oppressive, your son dead—what can you do?

Mr. Stevens, the band director, had found a place in the very last row of chairs, not covered by the canopy. He was wearing dark sunglasses, his green tweed jacket, and he'd trimmed his scraggly red-blond beard. He was older, maybe forty-five, maybe fifty, and scrawny. He looked like he was carrying the load of the world on his skinny shoulders. He looked beaten.

Mr. Stevens had been hired on as an assistant director at the high school six years back, and when the old band director retired, he took over. He loved jazz and the blues, couldn't get enough of the South Texas *conjunto* music since first he'd heard it one Saturday morning on a public radio station, and had all kinds of music playing in his office and over the speakers in the band hall when class wasn't in session.

One day three years ago, frustrated by his students' lack of enthusiasm for the piece they were taking to competition, he stopped a rehearsal midway, pulled out a couple of LPs and a record player from his office, and said to the students, "This is Miles Davis. Listen. It's his heart and soul. He's showing you the world's core through his music. The clay and fire. He's letting you in on its secrets, every one of them. That's how you need to be playing. . . . Now listen to this. It's Coltrane. . . ." He propped up the LP covers on the chalkboard railing behind him for his students to see.

One kid said, "This is Black music, man. You're a gringo, we're Hispanic. What's it have to do with you? Or us?"

"This isn't Black music. It's not even music. It's beyond music." They all stared at their teacher blankly. "It's hard to explain," he said, "but, wait—wait right here, okay?" He left the hall, and in a few moments returned with a CD. He didn't cut Coltrane off, just turned him down. It was still there, a buzz in the corner by the trumpet section. Then Stevens played Narciso Martinez. "See?" he said after a few moments. "Now do you hear it? The secrets are here, too. Like a heaviness. Can you hear the weight in the music? It's in the *bajo sexto* and the accordion." He closed his eyes and tapped the beat on his chest.

Some of the band members giggled, nervous that their director had lost his mind. The same kid from before said, "You think we're wetbacks, Stevens?" Some more students laughed.

But not PD.

He was still lost on Miles and Coltrane, especially Coltrane, shutting out all the noise: the kid complaining, Melissa next to PD blowing the spit out of her trumpet, Stevens talking, the others laughing. Just Coltrane now, buzzing somewhere in the corner, a raspy river of sound. Then Narciso and his accordion joined in. PD closed his eyes and imagined Coltrane and Narciso on a stage—the one a Black guy and the other a Mexican. Just two guys on a dark stage playing a sax and an accordion; then no Coltrane and no Narciso, just their music on the stage. Their sounds swirling together, and an explosion next, then the notes showering down on PD, who was standing in the middle of the stage now, crying and laughing. How

René Saldaña Jr.

can that happen? he wondered. The music, its heaviness, in his chest, a slush of tears in there, and laughter.

PD got what Mr. Stevens was saying. Stevens looked at the record player like he could see these same guys on stage too.

"It's about the music," he said, biting at his fingernails. "It's about their souls, our souls." He let Narciso play through to the end of the song.

Everyone stayed quiet until the song was over, then Stevens turned it all off. But PD got it stuck in his mind. It played in his ears the rest of the day, all through English II, Algebra I, history, on up to marching practice in the afternoon heat, where he was unable to concentrate on the steps he had already memorized, mucking it up for all of the marching band, forcing them to have to start over.

But Coltrane, man, he got to PD something fierce. And Narciso, too. He began to mix up the sax and the accordion. It was supposed to be Coltrane, his sound; instead, PD kept hearing the same music, Coltrane's, but coming out of Narciso's accordion. PD shook his head, and was somehow able to get through that afternoon's band practice.

Next day, Mr. Stevens heard music down the hall from his office, a trumpet, and for a second he thought it was somebody playing his record from yesterday. He sat on his clunky chair, heavy with the music, almost like he was drowning in a river rushing past. He got up finally, his eyes half closed as he walked, listening to the music. It was Coltrane he heard, but on a trumpet from one of the practice rooms. Stuff he'd heard before but never heard before, not quite like this, if you get what I mean. Harder, maybe like early Coltrane playing his older stuff, but on a trumpet. He walked through the empty hall. Beyond the hall. That's where it was coming from.

He walked to the practice rooms and saw through the glass it was PD, playing his trumpet, his back to the door, the door slightly ajar.

PD sitting there, his back to the world beyond the door, his head dipping to a beat.

Stevens imagined PD had his eyes closed, the boy's right knee rising and falling to that same beat. Then it was that Stevens noticed the boy playing the same song over and over, what he'd played to the students yesterday, and with it something else mixed in, that harder primal sound—those're the only words he could use to try to explain to himself the boy's playing: hard, base, basic, primal, crude, original, the world's soul exposed. He heard the accordion coming out of this boy's trumpet, and a sax. This boy, third-chair trumpet, a sophomore, good enough at playing and marching, not exceptional, but just good enough. Stevens couldn't understand this boy's playing right now.

Then PD turned, his trumpet on his lap, and looked at Stevens. "Sorry. I should go." PD had decided to skip English II. He began to put away his horn. "What's that you were playing? I mean, I know what it is, but . . ." He looked over PD's shoulder. "Where's your sheet music?"

"No sheet music. Playing from memory."

"From yesterday?"

The boy nodded.

"But it was such a short moment. You couldn't have—"

"It was long enough. That John Coltrane is good. And Narciso Martinez, also. You wouldn't think that they're so

René Saldaña Jr.

much alike, that they can say the same thing to you, being different like they are. But . . ."

"Yeah, you wouldn't know it at all. I mean to say, *most* people wouldn't know it. But you got it."

"I think so."

PD clasped shut his instrument case and left the band hall. Mr. Stevens walked back to his office, all the while shaking his head.

Two or three days later, Stevens loaned several CDs to PD. Some more jazz, some blues, a bit of classical, something that sounded foreign to PD, maybe Jewish. Lots more stuff. But PD didn't have a CD player, so he took one from a teacher's room, and he listened to all the music at home. For a week he kept the player and the music, and he couldn't sleep hardly. Then, before hopping on the bus to go to an away football game with the band that Friday afternoon, he handed back the music to Mr. Stevens. "Thanks," he said. Earlier, he'd snuck back to that teacher's room and replaced the CD player, right where he'd found it.

The following Monday, Mr. Stevens asked PD, "So? What did you think?"

"It's so clear. They're all telling me the same thing."

"What's that?"

"It's about suffering. More than that—the struggle. But the overcoming it too. I could hear the heaviness. It weighs a ton, man."

The two became fast friends. Dig it—an old white dude and a young Chicano kid. Who would've thought? I'm not saying they hung out at lunchtime or dared each other to go steal a soda from the corner store, or talked in secret about their girlfriends. Seeing them in class, you wouldn't even guess they knew each other except for in the band hall, as teacher and student. Stevens didn't promote PD to first chair, and PD didn't call Mr. Stevens by his first name, not in private, and definitely not in public. But they were good friends, the best.

PD's senior year, Stevens got PD a gig. That's what he called it, a gig. At some cafe downtown in McAllen. PD had been working on some of his own stuff this last year—Indio Blues, he called it. That night at the cafe, Stevens played a bit of the bass guitar—*toam-tum-tum*—a heartbeat that vibrated just underneath the tiled floor all the way to PD's feet, then up his legs and spine; and soon his own heart matched the tempo of the bass.

He was nervous—the lights all on him, his stomach vibrating from Stevens's bass—so he closed his eyes, put his trumpet to his lips, and played. Man, the first set he dragged out for close to a half hour, nonstop. But it wasn't the same song for that long. He'd take a deep breath and change directions, and Stevens had to play catch-up. When PD finished, Stevens stopped—dead cold, in the middle of some riff he was on; but it worked. You know how it is—you come to the end when the end comes. That's that.

PD was exhausted after two more sets just like the first one—sweaty, drooping at the shoulders, but blowing his Indio Blues solid, all the way through to the end.

Then he played every weekend at different places. Stevens backing him up, but most times he'd just quit playing the bass and listen. That's how good this kid was. Nobody cried because of his playing. He didn't bring people to their knees. Nobody fainted. But they heard it was their song he was playing, some

René Saldaña Jr.

people looking around to see if the others knew their secrets were being exposed in the notes. Embarrassed. But every one of them, their hearts in their throats. Happy and sad all at once.

This week, we lost—the bunch of us—we lost something of his music in PD's passing. Each of us some different note of his, but each just as heavy.

This afternoon, Stevens, under his sunglasses, cried. So did PD's family and friends. They cried because he was gone—no more of his early morning practicing on his horn, waking everybody in the whole house, in the entire neighborhood. Stevens cried because he'd heard PD play that first time in the band hall. He'd played behind him at the coffeehouses in town. Now, Stevens heard only the memory of the sound, reverberating, a buzz, the heartbeat of the soul of the world. His shoulders shaking under the load of it all. He cried, wondering if the memory was enough.

This afternoon, at the cemetery, the sun pounded down something fierce. A trying heat—and there was no tent big enough to keep it off us all.

HUM

by Naomi Shihab Nye

Sami Salsaa had thought things were improving in his new life, right before they got worse.

His classmates had stopped joking about his first name ending with "i," like a girl's name—Brandi, Lori, Tiffani. And about his last name, which they said sounded like hot sauce.

In a country where basketball stars had fish names—Kobe, Samaki—they could get over it. In a country where people poked silver posts through their tongues and shiny rings into their navels and the man at the auto body shop had a giant swan with a pink heart tattooed on his upper right arm, who cared?

His parents had taken his advice, which was rare.

"Don't call it 'America,'" Sami had said to them, after they unpacked their cracked suitcases on August 6, 2001, and settled into putty-colored Apartment 276 with the tiny black balcony jutting out over a stained parking lot. The sign at the bank across the street flashed 98 degrees. Sami hadn't realized Texas would be so blazing hot.

"Call it 'the United States,'" he said soberly. "'America' means more, means North, South, and Central America, the whole thing. Don't you like it better when people say 'Palestine' instead of 'the Middle East'? We shouldn't sound dumb."

They stared at him.

His mom said, "I only said 'America' because it was shorter."

Both of them started saying "United States" right away.

School in Texas started in the middle of August. Sami got an easy locker combination—10-20-30—and the best mark in his eighth-grade class on the first pre-algebra test of the year. Algebra was one of those subjects that translated easily from country to country; Sami had started working with equations in his cousin Ali's textbook in Bethlehem a year ago, during a curfew period, so the concepts felt familiar.

The teacher singled him out for praise, mentioning his "neatness" and "careful following of directions." Though he had not yet raised his hand once in class, now he thought he might. Sami found himself wishing he were taking full-fledged algebra instead of pre-algebra, which sounded babyish.

There was so much to look at in this country. Girls in tight T-shirts and jeans, for one thing. Magazines with interesting covers fanned out on a neat rack next to soft blue couches in the library's reading corner. Fifty different kinds of bread in neat plastic wrappers lined up at the grocery store.

Two boys, Gavin and Jim, set their trays down next to his at lunch. They told him what a corn dog was. They showed him how to dip it into a small pool of mustard. A girl named Jenny laughed when he tried it.

"Do you have brothers and sisters?" they asked.

"No," Sami said. "I am probably the only Palestinian who doesn't have any brothers or sisters." All his cousins and friends back home had huge families.

His history teacher asked him to stay after class during the third week of school and surprised him by saying, "I just want you to know I think our country's policy in your homeland has been very unfair. And more people than you might think would agree with me. Don't let the slanted press coverage get you down." The teacher clapped his hand on Sami's shoulder warmly and smiled at him.

Sami felt light walking the long sunny blocks between school and his apartment complex.

This might work out after all.

On top of that, his father flew to Los Angeles for the weekend to see his brother, Sami's uncle, and reported that hummus, Sami's favorite simple food from back home, was served on the plane. Incredible! Hummus, in a little plastic tub, with a shrink-wrapped piece of pita bread alongside it!

Next thing they knew, there might be a *falafel* stand in Lubbock.

It had been difficult for Sami's family to leave Bethlehem, the only town Sami and his mother had ever lived in, but the situation there had been so horrible recently, everyone was exhausted. Sami's school had been closed every other week and all citizens of Bethlehem put under curfew. His aunt Jenan had been gunned down in the street by Israeli soldiers as she returned from the market. When she died, it was the first time Sami ever felt glad she had no children. Always before, he had wished she had a boy just his age. His parents

Naomi Shihab Nye

cried so much they said they used up all their tears.

So when his father, a professor at Bethlehem University, was offered a teaching position in the engineering department at Texas Tech in Lubbock, he accepted it. Sami had felt sad at first that his family wasn't moving to a community with lots of other Arab immigrant families, like Dearborn, Michigan. Lubbock was a remote west Texas city with far fewer immigrants than Dallas or Houston. Someone on the plane told Sami's mother that a Middle Eastern bakery in Austin churned out spinach pies and *zaater* bread by the hour. That made Sami wish they were moving to Austin.

"Use this situation as an opportunity," his father said when Sami worried out loud about being too noticeable in Lubbock. His father always said things like that. "Let people notice you for how outstanding you are, not just how different."

A teacher at school told Sami there was an Arab family living far out on a ranch, raising cows. Their kids were in college already. This surprised Sami. Arabs knew about cows? He thought they only knew about sheep and goats. A famous Syrian eye surgeon had moved to Lubbock with his family long ago. Sami's father planned to go meet him soon.

Lubbock had a huge, straight horizon; it would be hard to find a larger horizon in the whole United States. You couldn't see a single hill in any direction. At night the stars glittered dramatically in the giant dark dome of sky. There were smooth streets in all directions with no Israeli tanks or armed soldiers in them, neat buildings and shopping centers, brilliant pink and orange sunsets, shiny pickup trucks with tires, and men in blue jeans wearing baseball caps that said COORS and RED RAIDERS.

"Hey, Sambo!" shouted one of his classmates outside the cafeteria a few weeks after school began. This made Sami feel familiar, jovial. He couldn't understand why the boy got in trouble for saying it.

Sami and his mother stood on the balcony and watched with pleasure as the sky swirled like milk in tea, one night before the dreadful day, when smoke poured from the buildings in New York and Washington and the buildings fell and the people died and no one was able to look at Sami in quite the same friendly way at school.

His parents had bought the television set just a few days before and kept checking out the different channels, so they had it turned on at breakfast when the news broke.

Sami wished he had never seen the images of the jets flying into the buildings.

He wished he had closed his eyes.

Before that morning, a soaring silver airplane had been Sami's favorite mental image; he'd always dreamed of the plane that would lift him out of a hard and scary life into a happier one, even before their big journey. Planes were magic; you stepped on, then stepped off in a completely different world. Someday he thought he'd go to New Zealand, and other places too. The world was a deep pocket of wonders; he had barely stuck his hand in.

But now Sami's joy in watching and imagining jets in flight was totally ruined.

He did not go to school. His father went to the university to teach a ten o'clock class, but none of his students appeared,

Naomi Shihab Nye

so he came home. Everyone was numb. Sami and his parents stared hard at the television all day. He knew his relatives and friends in Bethlehem would be watching too. Sami's eyes kept blurring. Each time the television voices said "Arabs," his heart felt squeezed. A reporter said Palestinians had been "celebrating" the disaster, and Sami knew that was a lie. Palestinians had practically forgotten how to celebrate anything.

He stood at the window staring out, feeling afraid some other terrible thing would drop from the sky and flatten everyone.

When it was eventually evening a tall man he had noticed before, walking slowly with a large blond dog on a leather harness, came around the corner on the level below, and paused.

The man turned and sat down in a green plastic chair next to a door on the ground floor. Was that his apartment? The dog stretched out beside him.

The man stared into the empty darkening sky and the empty blue water of the swimming pool. No one was swimming now. Why wasn't he watching television like everyone else?

That night Sami's mother forgot to cook. So Sami toasted bread in their new toaster oven and spread red jelly on top. It looked like blood. He offered bread to his parents, but they didn't want to eat.

He had never seen his parents so shocked before, not when Jenan died, not even when his own friends were beaten and shot by Israeli soldiers, or when his uncle's perfect stone house was bulldozed to the ground without any cause or recourse. *Sad,* Sami had always seen them, forever and ever—sadness was their tribal legacy—but this shocked? Never.

Although they had all been trying to speak only in English, to sharpen their English skills, they reverted to Arabic without even noticing it.

His parents stayed up almost all night, fixated on the screen, and Sami lay awake, shivering, staring at his ceiling. What made people do what they did?

The next day, his father met him outside the school to walk him home. "Did anything bad happen today?" his father asked.

Sami shook his head. Some students had stayed home for a second day. Teachers turned on television sets in the class-rooms. Everyone had been so shocked they forgot he was there.

A tight pressure in his chest made it hard to breathe.

Bad things started happening the *next* day, but Sami couldn't tell his parents.

"Go HOME," said a scribbled, unsigned note taped to his locker.

"Your people are murderers," Jake Riley whispered in homeroom.

Murderers? His people? No one had said the hijackers were Palestinian.

His family had always spoken out against the suicide bombings that killed Israeli civilians. Many Palestinians did. But who could hear them? They were regular people, not politicians. No one quoted them in the news.

All day Sami thought of things he might have whispered back.

Naomi Shihab Nye

Not true.

Just a few of them.

Some of yours are too.

A counselor came to take Sami out of class. She had a worried expression. "You realize that you are the only Arab student in this school at a very difficult time. If anyone gives you any trouble . . ."

Sami didn't think he could tell her what had already happened.

It would make him seem weak.

If anyone found out he told, they would hate him even more.

No one sat with him at lunch now. He tried sitting down next to some boys from his PE class and they stopped speaking and stared at him. "I feel very bad about what happened," Sami said, with difficulty, though his words were so true. "Very very bad." His tongue felt thick. But did saying that implicate him in some way? As if all Arabs had done it? Still, what else could he say?

Nobody answered him. They finished eating in silence, exchanging glances with one another, and left the table.

The streets of Lubbock glistened in their solitude for days and days. It seemed no one was going out to shop. Restaurants were empty. Everyone stayed glued to their gloomy televisions.

In English class Sami and his classmates wrote responses to September 11 for more than a week and read them out loud, discussing them at length. The teacher even insisted they do second drafts. She said it would be good therapy.

Sami was the only one who mentioned that other people in

the world also suffered from terrorism, all the time. Some of it, he said, was even governmentally sponsored and official. He did not mention his own family's bad experiences. He wrote this so that Americans wouldn't feel as if they were the only victimized people in history. But no one responded as if this had been a good thing to say.

Sometimes it seemed that a huge blanket had been spread over the vast and lumpy distant sorrows of the world—hushing them. Making them invisible. But weren't they still under there? Maybe people could only feel the things that touched *them,* the things at closer range.

One evening before sunset, Sami said to his parents, "I'm going out to take a walk."

"No!" his mother said. "It's almost dark!"

His father touched her hand to quiet her, and said, "Just around the apartments, yes? Don't leave the apartments."

His father looked so tired again, the way he had before they left Bethlehem. Some students had tried to drop his classes, though the deadline for that had passed.

A mysterious person had placed an ugly anonymous letter inside his faculty mailbox, but his father wouldn't tell Sami exactly what it said.

"Did you throw it away?"

"I burned it," his father said sadly. "In the outdoor ashtray."

Everyone had forgotten how to smile.

Sami's mother was working as an aide at a nursery school. She felt the eyes of the parents on her like hot buttons when they read her name tag, HANAN, even if they didn't know where she was from.

Sami stepped outside. He walked down the metal stairs

Naomi Shihab Nye

toward the vacant swimming pool. Trash cans were spilling over next to the barbecue grills.

A little toddler stood on a couch inside a neighboring apartment, staring out. Sami fluttered his fingers at her. She ducked and covered her face. The baby was lucky. She could not understand the news.

Cars slept in their assigned spaces under the carport roof. It seemed strange, but Sami felt jealous of them. It might be easier to be a car.

Another evening he asked his mother if he could make soup. She was surprised at his sudden interest in cooking. He rinsed lentils in a colander, as he had seen her do many times. He chopped an onion and fried garlic in a skillet.

As the soup was simmering, his mother remembered she had forgotten to pick up the mail downstairs when she came in from work. She asked if he would go get it and handed him the little key.

The mailbox was stuffed with bills and ads.

How could so many people have their address when they'd only been here two months?

Walking back toward the apartment with his hands full, Sami kicked a red balloon on the ground. It felt good to kick something sometimes. The balloon had a ribbon dangling from it—someone must have had a party. Today he had wished he could kick his backpack at school. Did those hijackers realize they had ruined his life too? He used to kick stones on the roads around Bethlehem. These were the same white stones that everyone was always getting in trouble for throwing. He only kicked them.

Once he had kicked a tin can all the way to Manger Square and his father passed him walking home from the bakery with a fresh load of steaming pita bread wrapped inside a towel. He spoke sharply to Sami for wasting his time.

"Find something useful to do," his father had said.

Today, so far away, after so much had happened, Sami thought of those long-ago words as the balloon snagged on a bush and popped. He spotted a thick unopened envelope on the ground. Had it fallen from someone's trash?

He stooped to pick it up, awkwardly, since his hands were full.

The envelope was addressed to Hugh Mason, Apartment 109.

Looking around, Sami realized that was the apartment where the tall man with the blond dog lived.

Sami pressed the buzzer. The man opened the door, dog at his side. He was staring straight ahead. Sami had finally understood, after watching him pass through the courtyard more than once, that he couldn't see. "Yes?"

The dog seemed to take a step forward to stand between his master and Sami.

"Mr. Hug Mason?" Sami pronounced it "hug"—he had never seen this English name before and did not know how to say it.

The tall man laughed. "Yes?"

"I have a letter for you with your name on it. I found it on the ground by the mailboxes. Maybe you dropped it?" He also wanted to ask, "How do you read it?" but was embarrassed to.

Mr. Mason put out his hand. "Thank you. I have dropped many things in my life. Very kind of you. You have an interesting accent. Where are you from?"

Naomi Shihab Nye

Sami hesitated. Could he lie?

Could he say Norway?

He knew his accent was not like a Mexican-American accent.

"I am," he said, in as American a voice as he could muster, "from Bethlehem."

Mr. Mason paused. "So you're Palestinian?"

"I am."

The dog seemed to have relaxed. He sniffed Sami's hand. His pale coat was lush and rumpled.

Mr. Mason's voice was gentle. "That must be harder than usual these days."

Sami felt startled when tears rose up in his own eyes. At least the man couldn't see them.

Sami whispered, "It is. Does your dog have a name?"

Half an hour later, Hugh and Sami were sitting on the green plastic chairs outside together, still talking. Tum Tum lay calmly beside them. They had discussed Lubbock, school, the troubles of Bethlehem, and the recent disaster. It was amazing how fast they had each talked, and how easily they had moved from subject to subject. They had not mentioned Hugh Mason's blindness, though Sami felt curious about it.

But they *had* discussed Tum Tum's job. Hugh had flown to California to be trained, alongside Tum Tum, four years ago. Training lasted twenty-eight days and was very "intense." Sami liked that word. He had never used it. This was Hugh's second dog. He'd had his first one for twelve years after his wife was killed. Killed? Crossing a street. "Hit-and-run." Sami didn't know the phrase. Hugh had to explain it.

Tum Tum had been trained for "intelligent disobedience."

If, for example, he saw Hugh getting ready to do something dangerous, like fall off a cliff (were there any cliffs in Lubbock?) or into the swimming pool, he would stand up on his hind legs, put his huge paws on Hugh's shoulders, and knock him over backward.

Later, thinking about it, Sami wished all people had dogs to guide their behavior if they were about to get into trouble.

When Tum Tum needed to go outside the apartment to pee behind a bush, he would hum.

Hum? What was "hum"? Hugh demonstrated, making a low smooth sound in his throat. Not all guide dogs did this—it was something particular to this one.

Tum Tum's ears perked up straight when he heard Hugh humming. Hugh said that if Tum Tum was just sitting on the grass right next to him, the dog would sometimes hum or make little talking sounds to let Hugh know what he was doing. Now he hummed in response to Hugh's hum. Tum Tum was a very communicative dog.

Hugh said that when a guide dog died, the loss for a blind person was nearly as hard as the loss of a human being, you were so used to each other by then. But had he always been blind? Why was this such a hard question to ask?

Sami heard his mother's worried call. The soup! He had forgotten it completely. He jumped up.

His mother walked anxiously toward them with her hands raised. What had happened to him?

Sami answered in Arabic.

This was a good man, he'd found a letter . . . but his mother only said in Arabic, "*Come home.*"

Sami said to Hugh, "Excuse me, we will visit another day?"

Naomi Shihab Nye

Hugh stood up and shook his hand as if Sami were a school principal.

"Anytime! I enjoyed the visit very much." He held out his hand in the general direction of Sami's mother and said, "Good evening, pleased to meet you, I am Hugh Mason, you have a very nice son."

The lentils were too soft. Sami measured cumin and salt into the pot. He squeezed lemons. His mother was anxiously waiting for his father to come home. She was fretting and dusting things. At dinner Sami's mother told his father, he *had been with a man,* as if it were a big mistake to talk to a neighbor!

Sami couldn't believe it.

"Did you go in his house?"

Sami knew better than to go in his house.

"No."

"What did he want from you?"

"Nothing! To talk! He can't even see!" For the second time that afternoon, tears rose into Sami's eyes. "He offered me a job."

"A JOB?"

A fork fell off the table.

"To read to him. He is very smart. He works at a hospital answering telephones. The phone board has a Braille panel so he can connect the calls. Someone drives him there. The dog goes too. Tum Tum. But he needs some reading help at home."

His father said, "You need to focus on your studies."

Sami said, "But he would pay me! I need some money too! Also, I learned new words. He has an excellent vocabulary, like a professor. I would read the newspaper, his mail, some magazines, and maybe even books. PLEASE?"

His father closed his eyes and shook his head. "Some days I wish we had never come here."

Sami started reading to Hugh on Tuesday and Thursday evenings. He read for two hours. Sometimes his throat felt hoarse afterward. He and Hugh sat outside when the weather was warm. When the "northers" came—Hugh told Sami that was the word everyone used for the cold winds from the north—they sat inside, Sami on the flowered couch and Hugh in a wooden chair at the table. Tum Tum sprawled happily between them and seemed to listen.

Sami would read the newspaper headlines and ask Hugh if he wanted to hear the stories. Whenever it was a sad story about Palestine and Israel, Hugh would say, "No. Don't read it. Tell me a story about Bethlehem instead."

So Sami would put the paper down and find himself describing little details he had never mentioned to anyone before. The way the stones were stacked to make a wall outside his old school. Crookedly, if you looked at it from the side. But the wall felt smooth along the top.

The olive-wood carvers who shaped elegant nativity sets and doves of peace from hunks of wood and served mint tea to traveling nuns, hoping they would buy presents to take home.

The teacher whose jacket was so old and raggedy he had long threads trailing down his back. Everyone whispered that he lived alone, had no one to take care of him. This was rare in Bethlehem. Few people lived alone. (Sami felt bad after telling this, since Hugh lived alone. No, not alone. He had Tum Tum.)

Sami told about the ancient wrinkled grandma-lady who made small date pies and kept them warm in her oven. She gave them to any student who stopped to visit her, even for two minutes, on the way home from school.

Hugh said he could visualize all these things with his "inner eyes."

"Does everyone have inner eyes?" Sami asked. "Even people who can see?"

"Of course," said Hugh. "You know whenever you remember something? You use them then. But some people don't use them enough. They forget about them. But they're all I have. In some ways, I think I can see better than people who aren't blind."

The teachers at school had urged Sami to join the Debate Club, but he didn't want to debate anyone. Debate involved winning and losing. Sami felt more attracted to "dialogue," a word he had heard Hugh use frequently, because dialogue was like a bridge. The teachers said, "In that case, you'll have to start your own club."

"Okay," he said. Why did he say that? he thought later. He didn't know how to start a club!

His history teacher printed up a set of "Guidelines for Dialogue Groups" off the Internet. It said things like: (1) Never interrupt; (2) Try to speak in specifics and stories, instead of generalities; (3) Respect varying opinions. Everyone does not have to agree, but everyone needs to respect everyone else.

A Korean girl named Janet approached Sami in the gym and said she had heard about the club from the art teacher and wanted to join it. "The art teacher is my good friend," Janet said. "Let's go to her room tomorrow after school and make some posters on those big tables."

Sami was glad Janet was so artistic since he was *not*. She designed the posters and he colored in the letters and graphics with fat felt-tip markers. Janet chattered freely as they worked. Adopted at birth, she had been brought to west Texas by her parents. Everyone was always asking her if she was Chinese.

The new club met on a Wednesday after school in the English classroom. Three students from Mexico City appeared at the meeting, looking quizzical. They said their English teacher had told them to come, to work on their language skills. They were happy to talk about anything. A tall Anglo American who had lived in Saudi Arabia with his oil engineer dad, an African-American girl named Hypernia, a very large girl in overalls, and a boy with a prosthetic leg appeared. Sami would never have known about the leg until the boy sat down and his pants revealed a bit of hardware at his ankle. There was also a Jewish boy who went by his initials, L. B.

For the first meeting, people just introduced themselves and told a bit about their lives. The boy who had lived in Saudi Arabia said he felt personally grieved by September 11, since the Arabs he had known were always so "nice." Hypernia said she had felt very lonely since her parents moved to Lubbock from Dallas, where she'd attended a school that was 80 percent African-American. "I feel like an alien or something. Like everyone is staring at me. I never felt this way before."

L. B. said he was really tired of explaining about the Jewish holidays. Sami asked if he had ever been to Israel and he said no, but his grandmother had. He stared at Sami hard and said, "I really wish people could get along over there. I mean, it's terrible, isn't it?"

Sami said, "*Really* terrible." He liked the boy just for saying that.

The club ended up talking about the Pakistani auto mechanic on the east side of town whose shop windows had been broken after September 11. It had been in the newspaper. They decided to go visit him, take him a card.

Janet suggested "On Not Fitting In" as a topic for their next meeting. She had brought a poem by James Wright, an American poet, to read. It said, "Whatever it was I lost, whatever I wept for / Was a wild, gentle thing, the small dark eyes / Loving me in secret. / It is here."

Sami found it mysterious, but it made him think of Tum Tum.

He mentioned to the group that he worked for a man who could not see in usual ways, but who might be a nice guest speaker for their group someday. He had interesting ideas, Sami said, and he liked to listen. "I'm visually impaired too," said the large girl in overalls. "Bring him. I'd like to meet him." Sami looked at her, surprised. He had seen her tilt her head to other people as they spoke, but had no indication she was blind. Suddenly he noticed the white cane on the floor at her side. She said softly, as if in answer to a question he didn't ask, "I only see shades of light and dark. But I can't see any of your faces."

Weeks went by. The Dialogue Club was featured on the morning announcements at school. Gavin, who had once, so long ago, eaten lunch in the cafeteria with Sami, came to the club to write a story for the school paper, and he didn't get a single fact or quote wrong, which amazed the club members. They said the school paper was famous for getting everything wrong.

Sami's parents invited Hugh to dinner. They had stopped worrying about Sami's job when they discovered how nice and smart Hugh was. Sami's father seemed to feel a little embarrassed about having acted so negative in the beginning. So he took care to ask Hugh many questions, including the one Sami was most curious about himself.

Hugh had lost his sight at the age of four to hereditary glaucoma, a disease that could have been partially averted if he'd had surgery earlier. His mother always blamed herself afterward for not realizing what was happening to her son. No one she had known in her family or his father's family had this condition. But she had known that Hugh, as a tiny boy, had vision troubles, and had gotten him thick glasses and fussed at him for stumbling instead of taking him to medical experts when something could still have been done. This great sorrow in the family eventually led to a divorce between Hugh's parents.

"So you went to college—when you were already blind?" Sami's father asked gently.

"Yes, I did. And there I met the woman who eventually married me, my wife, Portia. She was African-American, and her parents never forgave her for marrying someone white *and* blind—it was too much for them. But we had nine wonderful years together. You would have liked her, Sami."

Sami's eyes were wide open. How many kinds of difficulties there were in the world that he had not even imagined yet!

His parents played soft Arabic flute music on their little tape player in the background for the first time in months, and served grape leaves, cucumber salad with mint and yogurt, and *ketayef*—a crescent-shaped, nut-stuffed pastry with honey sauce. Hugh ate a lot, and said it was the best meal he had tasted in *years*. Sami had seen the cans of simple soup lined on his kitchen counter, the hunks of cheese in the refrigerator, the apples in a bowl. He watched Hugh eat with gusto now and noticed how his fork carefully found the food, then his mouth, without any mishap or awkwardness.

Tum Tum kept sniffing the air as if he liked the rich spices.

Once he hummed loudly and Sami's father laughed out loud, for the first time since September 11. "What is that? Is he singing?"

Sami rose proudly to open the door to the courtyard. "It's his language," Sami said. "He needs to be excused for a moment."

He knew Tum Tum would walk to his favorite bush and return immediately, scratching on the door to be let back in. And he would not get the apartment doors confused, though they all looked alike—Tum Tum always knew exactly where Hugh was, instinctively. Sami's dad shook his head. "In this country, even dogs are smart."

Hugh said, "Friends, my stomach is full, my heart is full. Sami, come over here so I can pat your black hair! I'm so happy we're neighbors!"

Now Sami laughed.

"Hugh," he said, "my hair is red."

Naomi Shihab Nye

EPIPHANY

by Ellen Wittlinger

On the first day of first grade, Epiphany Jones became my best friend. She had just moved to Bristol that summer and didn't know anybody yet, which was lucky for me. That was our first year of sitting at desks, and we had one of those alphabetizing teachers, so I, DeMaris Kanakis, sat right behind Epiphany Jones.

I could hardly believe there was actually a girl like Epiphany in my school. In kindergarten I had to hang out with the boys—who sometimes acted dumb as doorknobs, but at least enjoyed a good argument—because the girls in my class were just too girly. At recess they'd cluster around the teacher and try to hold her hand. I couldn't figure out what was wrong with them. They never seemed to have an idea more exciting than trading lunch box sandwiches.

But Epiphany and I were on the same page. For six years we made Kimball Elementary School a fun place to be—at least it was fun for us. We did everything bigger and longer and louder than anybody else, boys included. We built gigantic science projects that almost worked; we sang higher than anybody else in the chorus; we talked so much we had to be de-alphabetized; we bloodied our noses and broke our bones (once I broke one of Jack Glover's, too); and our favorite teacher (Mrs. Tolliver, fourth grade) said it broke her heart to see us move on to fifth. Kimball was a small school, so teachers from the next year would see us in the hallway and say, "DeMaris and Epiphany! I'm waiting for you!" We'd just laugh.

For our sixth-grade graduation, Epiphany and I got matching dresses. Even our mothers didn't know about it—it was a well-planned scheme. The dresses were bright blue, so you could see them quite well even from the back of the auditorium where our parents were sitting. When I won the Attendance Award, Epiphany stood up with me, and when she won the Best Speller Award, I stood up with her, arm in arm, as if we were locked together. Even though the prissy girls rolled their eyes, plenty of people thought we were funny. That's all it took to keep us going.

Unfortunately, Epiphany's parents did *not* think we were funny. They weren't too crazy about me, or Kimball Elementary, or the whole town of Bristol, I guess. They'd moved here for her dad's job, but as soon as school got out her parents would pack Epiphany and her brother off to spend the summer in Tennessee with their aunt and uncle and cousins. Epiphany didn't mind, because there were lots of kids to play with there, and I guess they were almost as much fun as I was. But I hated the summers when she was gone; they were long and boring. I killed time by becoming the cartwheel champion of Bristol and never walked anywhere I

Ellen Wittlinger

could cartwheel instead. It was something to do while I waited for Epiphany to come back.

Two days before the start of seventh grade, Epiphany returned from Tennessee and called me up.

"Hey," she said. "I'm back."

"Thank the Lord," I said. "Come over here right now. We have to figure things out!"

"Whataya mean, 'figure things out'?" she said. This was my first clue that something was wrong, but I tried to ignore it. Epiphany *always* knew what I meant without having to ask. We had practically the same brain.

"You know," I said. "Like, what to wear on the first day, and what kind of book bag to bring—this is junior high, you know. And bring your schedule over so we can see what classes we have together and which teachers."

She gave a big sigh as if I'd asked her to do something hard. "Okay, but I'll have to come tomorrow."

"Tomorrow hardly gives us any time!" I protested. "We need to make plans!"

"DeMaris, I don't intend to start junior high school wearing the same exact outfit as you, you know. We're not children anymore."

For a minute I didn't know what to say, which hardly ever happens. "I know we aren't. I'm not saying dress *identically*. I'm just saying, talk about it."

"I already know what I'm wearing," Epiphany said. "My cousin and I talked about it this summer. But if you want me to come over tomorrow to help you, I will."

It was the beginning of things going crooked between us.

Still, being at the junior high was exciting enough for me

to overlook it for a while. There are six elementary schools in Bristol that all go to the junior high, so every class was full of strange faces. I even loved the hallways—no more little kids bumping into you or crying or yelling. Here people leaned against their lockers and had low, important conversations with each other, like grown-ups. Some of the teachers even called us "Miss" or "Mister," which cracked me up every time.

The downside was that Epiphany and I had no classes together. After the first few days of newness wore off, I missed her terribly. When a teacher said something really dumb, there was nobody to look at and make faces with. Of course, we'd meet in the cafeteria for lunch and make jokes about the awful food before we built towers out of the mashed potatoes and stuck little corn windows all over them or made a house out of mystery meat and thatched the roof with coleslaw.

I started noticing, though, that Epiphany's heart wasn't really in it. Sometimes I'd catch her staring over at this big round table in the corner of the cafeteria where all the black kids usually ate. There were more black kids at the junior high than one table's worth, but not too many more, and the extra people just pulled chairs from other tables and squeezed in tight.

One day I asked Epiphany, "Do you wish you could eat with them instead of me?" I only asked this because I was absolutely sure that she'd laugh at me and say, "Are you crazy?" But she didn't. She stuck two fingers in her potato pile and said quietly, "Sometimes."

If you haven't figured it out yet, Epiphany is black and I am white. It never seemed to matter to her when we were at Kimball, where she was the only black kid, but at the junior high there were others, and it seemed like there was

Ellen Wittlinger

some kind of gravity pulling her over to them.

So I decided to be cool about it. "Well," I said. "You could eat with them sometimes."

"Who would you eat with?" Epiphany asked me.

"I don't know," I said, looking around the big room. "Maybe her." I pointed to a girl I recognized from my English class who was sitting alone at a table, reading a book.

Epiphany nodded. "Well, maybe someday I will then. Thanks." She looked at me sideways, sort of embarrassed, a look I'd never ever seen on her before. My stomach was balled up like I'd just eaten glue, but I smiled back at her, hoping "someday" would never come.

But it did. All that year Epiphany went back and forth between my table and the big table where the black kids ate. I got to know the girl who read books. Her name was Holly Lembach and she was more fun than she looked like at first, but she did not have the same brain I did, and she often didn't know what I meant, and most of the time we were not on the same page.

I felt sad the whole year. Even my mother noticed that I wasn't my usual cheery self. "Have you had an argument with Epiphany?" she asked. "She doesn't come over as much as she used to."

When I said we hadn't, Mom said, "Sometimes friendships change when you get older. You make new friends."

It was just some of that usual mother talk to make you feel better, but I wasn't in the mood for it. "I don't want to make any new friends!" I yelled at her, then slammed the door to my room so the discussion could not continue.

The summer before eighth grade, Epiphany went down to

Tennessee again. In a funny way I didn't mind so much. I mean if she was in Tennessee, just like every other summer, I could make myself believe nothing had changed—that we were still best friends. It was when she was here in Bristol, sitting across the cafeteria from me, that I wasn't so sure.

Holly and I were hanging around together a lot by then. She liked having sleepovers where we read magazines and tried out new hairstyles on each other. It was kind of girly, but I actually didn't mind as much as I thought I would. Holly turned thirteen two weeks before I did. To celebrate, her parents took us to a theater in Boston to see *Rent,* and then we went out for dinner to an expensive restaurant and ordered salmon. We both wore makeup and high heels. It was the most grown-up kind of celebration I'd ever been to, and I started thinking maybe Holly was just as much fun as Epiphany.

Still, a few days before school started, I called the Joneses' house.

"Oh, DeMaris," Mrs. Jones said, sounding a little aggravated, as usual. "Epiphany isn't home now."

"But she's back from Tennessee?" I said.

Her mother paused, then said simply, "Yes, she is."

I asked her to have Epiphany call me when she got back, but I never got a call. It made me mad that her mother didn't give Epiphany my message. What did I ever do to her?

I didn't see her until the first day of school, in the cafeteria. Holly and I were already in line when Epiphany came in with a group of black kids. I waved at her.

"Save my place," I told Holly, and ran over to hug Epiphany. But when I got close and saw the look on her face, I knew a hug would not be appreciated. Over the summer her

Ellen Wittlinger

looks had changed. Suddenly she had breasts, which were on display under a tight tank top, and her wild hair, which she'd always tied back with scarves or up with ribbons, was cropped to half an inch all around her head.

"Hey," she said, without smiling.

"Hey," I said, feeling Epiphany's new friends' eyes on me. "I called you. Didn't you get my message?"

She studied her elbow. "I got it."

"Oh." How could we have a conversation under such scrutiny? "Holly is saving my place at the front of the line. Do you want to eat with us?"

As soon as I asked the question, I knew the answer. One of the tall black boys snickered.

"I don't think so," Epiphany said. "I'll see you around, though."

"Okay," I said, and watched her turn away, her new pack of friends surrounding her like she was a magnet and they were nails. I was so angry I felt like crying, but instead I ranted to Holly.

"Epiphany is such a snob now! She acts like we were never even friends! She has to do everything with *those* kids."

Holly shrugged. "That's just how it is. They stick together. We stick together."

"But *why*?" I really wanted to know, but Holly was no expert.

"That's just how it *is*," she repeated. "I like Epiphany too, but I don't think she'll be eating lunch with us anymore."

"Well, that's just stupid," I said. "Just plain stupid."

Holly gave me half of her lemon square, to cheer me up.

For weeks I ate my lunch with one eye on the black kids'

table. Everybody was crazy about Epiphany, you could tell. Which made me remember why I liked her too. She could crack you up with a sideways look and then keep you laughing until you were too weak to breathe. When Epiphany was your friend, you felt special, even if everybody else thought you were weird. I couldn't believe she wasn't my friend anymore—it didn't make any sense.

"DeMaris, are you listening to me?" Holly said one day.

I focused my attention on her. "What? Sorry."

"I said I can't go to the movies with you on Saturday night this week."

"How come?" We'd gotten into a habit of going every weekend, unless the movies were really bad.

She smiled oddly. "This guy asked me to go to the dance."

"What dance?" I asked. "What guy?"

"There's a dance here, at school, on Saturday night. I swear, you don't pay attention to anything anymore, except *that table*. A guy in my algebra class asked me to go. Rick Saloman."

"Oh." I was caught off guard. A guy? Somehow it hadn't occurred to me that Holly was thinking about guys. But I guess most girls were. Even I had to admit that some of my old kindergarten friends had grown into good-looking guys. I just didn't have a clue what to do about it.

Holly pointed Rick Saloman out to me. He was sitting at a table full of boys, one of whom was pretending to choke so he could spit out his soda dramatically and make a big mess. Not Rick, though. He looked decent. When he saw us looking, he waved.

By the next Monday we had a new addition to our lunch table. Rick and Holly sat next to each other, rubbing shoulders and sharing french fries. They talked about the dance they'd gone to on Saturday, and the movie they saw together on Sunday afternoon—the movie I *hadn't* seen. I ate my own french fries and tried not to look at them.

Rick had class in the other direction from Holly and me, so when I got her alone, I said, "Is he always going to eat with us now?"

"He's my boyfriend, DeMaris. I *have* to eat lunch with him!"

"Already he's your boyfriend? That was fast."

"Listen," she said. "Having lunch with you is like eating alone anyway. All you do is stare at Epiphany. Why don't you just go over there and eat with them!"

It was an idea that had never occurred to me. Just go over and eat with them. Could I do that? "Maybe I will!" I told Holly. "Then you and your boyfriend can grin at each other like idiots without an audience."

She stalked away.

I started getting nervous by third period on Tuesday. Should I ask permission to sit there or just plunk my tray down like I belonged? I'd have to get there early enough to get a seat by Epiphany, but not too early in case I didn't know the other kids at the table. By the time I got myself through the lunch line (and noticed Holly and Rick already seated at a table for two), I'd decided not to think about it anymore—to just do it.

I waited until I saw Epiphany sit down next to a girl from my gym class named Lena, then I hurried over and pulled up a chair on her other side, slapped my tray on the table, and smiled.

"Hi, Lena. Hi, Epiphany." I took a bite of burger and looked past my onetime best friend to speak to Lena. "Do you think we'll have to do rope climbing in gym again today? My hands are still sore from yesterday. You got even farther up than I did."

Both of them were staring at me, Epiphany with narrowed eyes.

Finally Lena spoke. "Um, yeah, my hands hurt too."

By then a group of boys had joined the table. It was getting full and kids were pulling up chairs to crowd in. Every new person who arrived stared at me, but nobody said a word. The only other person at the table whose name I knew was this guy Theon from my history class, so I smiled at him, too. "Hi, Theon! How're you?"

Silence. Big, awful silence. Man, it was like wearing a Yankees hat in Fenway Park. I felt like I'd walked into a funeral parlor where everybody knew the dead guy but me. People chugged their lunches and left, some of them glaring at me like I was the plague, most ignoring me completely. When Epiphany was done, she stood up and looked down at me.

"I need to talk to you, DeMaris."

"Okay." We dumped our trays and headed for the door. Epiphany didn't say anything until we were outside the building and around the corner, out of sight of almost everybody.

"What do you think you're doing?" she asked me, straight out. She was madder than I'd ever seen her, but I stayed calm.

"Eating lunch with you," I said.

"Well, you can't eat at that table."

"Why not? It's a free country."

"That's what you think." Epiphany put her hands on her

Ellen Wittlinger

hips and surveyed me as though I were a new species instead of an old friend. "What happened to Holly? I thought you ate with her."

"She's got a boyfriend. They want to be alone."

Epiphany rolled her eyes—she is the best eye roller I know. "Well, I'm sorry, DeMaris, but you cannot eat at our table!"

"Why?"

"Because it makes everybody uncomfortable. Can't you tell that?"

"Yes. But I still don't know why. We were best friends for six years. How come all of a sudden you can't even sit at a lunch table with me?" Just saying it out loud made the sadness bunch up at the back of my throat, making my voice sound thick.

Epiphany leaned in close, as though she was going to tell me a secret. She laid her arm next to mine. "Because you are white, DeMaris, and I am black. Very simple."

I pulled my arm away. "Oh. And when we were in first grade and third grade and sixth grade, you weren't black then? I wasn't white then?"

"How can I make you get it?" she said, sighing. "Black kids need to stick together when we get older. You can't understand us. We're just too different now."

"We've still got two legs, two arms, two eyes, and big mouths—just like we always did. The only thing that's different now is your boobs are bigger."

She stamped her foot. "You aren't even trying to understand. DeMaris, do you see how many black kids there are at this school?"

"Yeah, pretty many."

"Pretty many? You think a dozen is pretty many?"

"Well, that's more than there were at Kimball."

"Which is why my parents hated Kimball so much."

"But you didn't hate it. We had fun there! I'm not saying you shouldn't have black friends too, but how come, all of a sudden, I don't even exist?"

"Because things change!" Her voice got kind of quiet. "We're not little kids anymore, DeMaris. We live in a bigger world now. I'm not saying it's your fault—that's just how it is between black people and white people. You just have to accept it." Her mouth curled down at one corner in a sad smile, and then she turned and walked away.

Of course, Epiphany should have known—I'm not the "accepting" kind.

On Wednesday I got to the table before she did. Theon and a couple of other boys were there, and one other girl I didn't know. I smacked my tray down, but kept standing.

I looked at Theon. "Why is it such a big deal if I want to eat here?"

Every one of them stared at me until I was starting to feel like you do in those dreams where you're up on stage and suddenly you realize you're naked. Finally Theon leaned way back in his chair and said, "'Cause you can eat at any table you want to."

I took a deep breath. "No I can't," I said. "I don't know most of these kids, and the ones I do know, I don't like very much."

The girl laughed, but it wasn't a nice laugh. "You don't know us, either. How come you think you like us so much?"

"She's one a them wanna-bes," another boy said. "We so

Ellen Wittlinger

cool, she thinks our cool blackness gonna rub off on her, she start getting darker and darker."

Just as they were all laughing at that hysterical idea, Epiphany showed up.

I pointed to her and watched her eyes get huge and round. "She's the reason I want to sit here. I know her as well as I know myself—she was my best friend for six years. Why do I have to give her up now just because I'm not black?"

Epiphany turned around and walked away. She dumped her whole tray of crappy food in the trash and marched right out of the cafeteria.

"Now that was just plain wasteful," Theon said. There was a low murmur of laughter, but most of the kids just stared at their plates. Lena had been standing behind Epiphany, watching the whole thing. She dropped her tray on the table and said, "You gonna eat standing up, girl?"

"Can . . . can I sit here?"

"You just told us you could, didn't you?"

So I sat. After a minute, the kids started talking to each other. Nobody said anything else to me, but at least they weren't all silent like the day before. And they weren't talking about anything especially *black,* as far as I could tell. I understood every single thing they said.

On Thursday Epiphany was waiting for me at the bottom of the cafeteria stairs. "Are you planning on ruining my life again today?" she said.

"Are you planning on throwing your lunch away and making a big scene?"

"Why are you doing this to me?" she wailed.

She sounded so upset, it made me feel terrible too. "I'm not doing it to hurt you, Epiphany! I just *miss* you!"

She turned away and looked up the stairs for a long time. Then she said, "Oh, what the hell. Come on."

By the time we got to the table everybody else was there and we had to squeeze in on either side of Theon. He and another boy were arguing about something.

"You think that Richards guy gonna give you a part, man? You wasting your time, Stokes. He doing Shakespeare, brother. He don't want no black Romeos."

A couple of kids looked over at us as we sat down, but the conversation continued.

"It's not *Romeo and Juliet* anyway," the boy called Stokes said. "It's *A Midsummer Night's Dream*. It's cool. I saw it last summer with my parents."

"I've seen it," Lena said. "You could be the guy who gets turned into a jackass."

"Oh, that is definitely the part that Richards guy will like you for, Stokes, man. A big black jackass." Theon put his head back and laughed like one himself.

"I'm going to the play auditions too," I said. "At three o'clock, right?"

The conversation came to a crashing halt. Suddenly turkey burgers were being devoured.

Then Stokes said, "Yeah, three o'clock."

I nodded. "Anybody else going? Epiphany, you should try out. You'd be great."

Another silence. But then Theon spoke up. "What's your name again, girl? Something weird, I know."

"DeMaris," I said. "DeMaris Kanakis."

"That's a mouthful," Lena said.

Theon continued. "DeMaris Kanakis, maybe you don't know it, but Mr. Richards, the drama teacher, don't like black people. He wouldn't put one a us in his damn play if his hair was on fire and we had the hose."

"Why do you think that?" I asked.

"'Why do you think that?'" Theon repeated in a high, silly voice.

"He thinks that," Epiphany said, "because when Theon took the drama class last year, Mr. Richards wouldn't let him use street talk when he was doing scenes. Like: *To be or not to be: dat bees da question.*"

Lena chuckled, but Theon looked furious. "You disrespecting me in front of this white girl, Epiphany?"

"Just saying what I know." She sucked her milk through the straw.

Theon glared at me. "You know what that Richards fool said to me? He said, 'Theon, you talk like a criminal!' That's what he said! *'Theon, you talk like a criminal!'* Who the hell he think he is, saying something like that? I ain't no criminal."

The tableful of people murmured agreement.

"I know," Stokes said. "T. J. had a bad story about him too—he's not cool, but I want to try out anyway. I want to show that damn guy I can act!"

"Anyway, Theon," I said. "Mr. Richards probably didn't know you can speak as well as anybody else when you want to."

Theon's eyes got big as Epiphany leaped out of her chair, grabbing my arm with one hand. "Let's go, DeMaris. I knew something like this would happen. You just don't *get* it!"

She was still explaining to me what it was I didn't get after school, when we went to the play auditions. She was still sort of mad, but I was so glad she was trying out for the play with me, I didn't mind too much.

"What you don't understand, DeMaris, is that talking like that *is* talking well, as far as Theon is concerned. As far as a lot of us are concerned. It's *our* language, just for us."

"You don't talk that way."

"Not in front of you. But I do sometimes, when I want to."

"But it makes white people think you want to be different," I said.

"We're treated different anyhow—we might as well flaunt it. Be proud of it!"

"You weren't different from me before," I said, but Epiphany wasn't listening. She was determined to teach me a few things, then and there.

"You can't say stuff like that to Theon—or anybody who's black—because *you're not*. And don't try to explain other white people to us, like we're too stupid to understand. If you're gonna come and eat with us, shut up and listen for a while, until you start to get how it is. Otherwise nobody is gonna say one word in front of you."

"But I didn't say Theon was stupid. I said just the opposite!"

"You think you did, DeMaris, but believe me, that's not how it sounded to us."

I sighed. "Is it always going to be like this now? You're part of an *us* and I'm not?"

She shrugged and sighed, but then her mouth turned up a little bit at the corner. "You're sitting at the damn table, aren't you?"

The auditions lasted almost three hours—there were at least sixty kids trying out, and Mr. Richards had us each read

Ellen Wittlinger

several parts. Epiphany and I got better and better every time we had to read; I knew bigmouthed crazy girls like us would be great actors. Stokes was there too; I watched Mr. Richards's face when Stokes read parts to see if I could catch him being prejudiced, but I decided it might not show right out front where I could see it. I did notice that he never looked directly *at* Stokes, the way he did the other boys. I bet Stokes noticed too. I knew Theon would have.

That night, for the first time in almost six months, Epiphany called me on the phone, and we laughed about all the stuff that had happened at the auditions. I was so happy I could hardly sleep.

Friday morning I ran to school. Mr. Richards had told us the callback list would be posted outside the theater door. If your name was on the list you were pretty sure to get a part, but you'd have to stay after school again for more auditions. I could see Epiphany standing at the board as I ran down the hallway.

"Did we make it?"

She whirled around and gave me a hug. "Of course we did! We are the best!"

After we danced around a minute, I looked at the list, just to see my name for myself. "Look! Stokes made it too! What do you think Theon will say now?"

Epiphany's smile folded into a grim line. "I don't know, but whatever he says, don't you say anything back! You hear me?"

"I know, I know—just listen."

And, boy, did I listen. Theon was going on about how Mr. Richards was gonna make fools out of Stokes and Epiphany, how he'd never give them decent parts because he was a racist. Then Epiphany said that, well, maybe he *was* a racist, she didn't know, but he was also the director of the play, so she expected he'd give the best parts to the best people. And then Lena said if he was a racist he might not be able to see who was best because he'd be blinded by his prejudices, and then Theon said why would black people even want to be in a play with a racist directing it, and then Stokes said because the world was full of racists and you couldn't just hide from them—you had to show them they were wrong, and then Theon called Stokes an idiot. I just sat and listened and hoped Epiphany was proud of me.

Once we got on stage again that afternoon, I just knew we were going to get good parts. A lot of the other girls seemed scared to death they'd make a mistake. Their voices were too small, they stood in one spot like they were nailed to the floor, and they looked ready to bust out crying half the time. Epiphany and I were just having fun, the way we always did.

Over the weekend we talked on the phone twice; once she called me and once I called her. We made plans to meet at the drama board first thing Monday morning to see what parts we'd gotten. We kept squealing to each other until her mother told her to stop making that awful noise. Her mother would probably have made an awful noise too, if she'd known who her daughter was talking to.

When Epiphany and I walked up to the lunch table Monday, we held our heads up like queens. Epiphany actually *was* a queen: Titania, queen of the fairies! And I got the part of Helena, one of the mixed-up lovers. Both of these are really good parts, and we were jumpy with excitement. Lena congratulated us first, and everybody else did too, except Theon, who just shook his head like we were all crazy. But we weren't the real stars. Turns out Stokes got the part of Puck, which is the biggest and best role of all. Puck is this mischievous forest imp who gets to leap all over the stage and play tricks on people. Stokes was so amazed, he couldn't believe it.

"So, what do you think now, Theon?" he said.

Theon snorted. "Doesn't prove anything. I still say, you better not turn your back on Richards. He's white, and don't you forget it."

Lena and Stokes glanced at me sideways. Epiphany frowned into her sandwich. I knew she didn't want me to say anything, but there are times you just can't keep your mouth shut.

"*I'm* white," I said.

Theon let his mouth drop open. "No kidding?"

Epiphany poked me with her sneaker, but I moved my foot away. "So, does that automatically mean you don't trust me?"

Theon squirmed a little in his chair, but he looked me right in the eye. "If you're white and I don't know you, I don't trust you."

I nodded. "Okay, but if you got to know me, you might trust me?"

"And how would I be gettin' to know you?"

"Maybe we could eat lunch at the same table," I said, smiling. Stokes stifled a laugh.

Theon rolled his eyes; he's almost as good at it as Epiphany. "You," he said, pointing at me and shaking his head. "You. I don't know. I don't know."

"Like, is there a ten percent chance, you think, or more than that?" I said.

Theon looked like he was trying hard not to laugh, but Lena let out a hoot.

"DeMaris Kanakis, I like the way you say things straight out," she told me.

I smiled. "So, it's not such a terrible thing that I came to sit at your table, huh?"

Theon let his head fall into his hand and actually smiled. Epiphany wrapped her leg around mine and said, "I knew you were crazy from the first minute I saw you, DeMaris. The very first minute."

A few weeks later, Holly dumped Rick Saloman. She pulled me aside in the lunch line. "Do you think they'd let me eat at the black table too?" she asked me.

"I think it's the black-and-white table now," I said.

When she sat down I introduced her to Lena and Stokes and some of the other kids. They mostly said, "Hey," like it was no big deal.

Then Theon said, "Holly? What kinda name's that supposed to be? Like a holly *bush*? Damn, I wouldn't stand for my mother naming me after no bush."

Holly stared Theon in the eyes. "I like my name. It's very . . . green."

Theon's eyes got big. "Oh, no, this one thinks she's *green*! We turnin' into a damn rainbow coalition!"

"Stranger things have happened," Epiphany and I said, simultaneously, then squealed with laughter.

We were back.

Ellen Wittlinger

BLACK and WHITE

by Kyoko Mori

By the time I was seventeen, a high school junior, I had forgotten a lot about my first eight years in Kobe, Japan. My
mother did not encourage me to speak Japanese. At home, she
did not cook Japanese food or listen to Japanese music. We
lived on a dairy farm in Wisconsin with my stepfather, Don.
Neither of my two stepsisters were at home: Caroline was at
college three hours away, and Tracy had graduated high
school in May and gotten married in June.

After Tracy left, I painted the beige walls of our bedroom lipstick pink, tore down the cream-colored curtains
my mother had sewn and hung in their place an Indian cot-
ton sheet picturing a Tree of Life surrounded by peacocks,
elephants, tigers, and monkeys, and put up all the posters I
liked but Tracy hadn't. My room looked like the room of
any teenage girl at our school. But there was a mirror
inside the closet door, and in it, I could see my straight
black hair cut shoulder-length, high cheekbones, and a
small nose with no ridge at the top so that every pair of

sunglasses slid off my face. My dark brown eyes were narrow and long instead of round, and my mouth no larger than a peach pit. Every feature of my face was too delicate. I was always startled to see this fragile-looking girl staring back at me, dressed in the clothes I shared with my best friend Mandy O'Brien.

Mandy's hair was almost as black as mine, and she was only an inch taller. We wore each other's flannel shirts, T-shirts, sweaters, and sweatshirts with the boys' size 13 Levi's from Sears. In the winter we traded our coats every week because each of us had only one—mine was a purple down parka and hers a black-and-red tartan wool flannel—and this way, it would take us twice as long to get sick of two coats instead of one. From a distance, we looked like twins. Week to week, no one could remember which one of us wore which coat. Each morning as I shut the closet door and headed out for school, I thought I was leaving behind that lone fragile-looking girl trapped in there, with all the prissy dresses, blouses, and skirts my mother had sewn that I no longer wore except to church.

Even though my mother grumbled about my boyish clothes, she should have been glad to see me dressed the same as other kids. She was the one who cautioned me against sticking out like an unruly nail waiting to be hammered down. "We're foreigners, after all," she said. "You have to be very careful not to call attention to yourself. If your friends get into trouble, people will think they were acting like rebellious teenagers. With you, it'll be different. People will blame you— and me, too—for being ignorant foreigners."

Up till the fall of my junior year, I hadn't done anything

for people to talk about. I ran on the cross-country team, volunteered for food drives and bake sales and highway cleanup projects, and made good grades. I wanted, like Caroline, to be one of the few girls from my class to go on to college. I made friends with other college-bound girls and avoided parties where kids got drunk or worse in someone's basement.

Maybe my mother didn't know it, but my good behavior came from a desire to be like Caroline, not from any uneasiness about being a foreigner. I had gone out for cross-country and joined the nature club because of the mornings I used to run and bird-watch with Caroline. In a marsh near our house that was protected by the state's wetland preservation project, Caroline had taught me to be quiet and attentive. She showed me how to recognize the red flicker of a cardinal's flight or the wavering pattern—like a musical score—that a flock of finches made in the air. Even after she left home, I often went to the marsh to sit alone, wait for birds, and think.

I attended school in a nearby town, North Holland, which had a public grade school, middle school, and high school—three small buildings in a block-long compound with a shared yard. I had moved there in the middle of second grade, when my mother left my father in Japan and came to Wisconsin to marry Don. They'd met in Kobe while he was visiting a cousin who taught English there. Even though I was the only person who hadn't gone to kindergarten in town, by high school I knew everyone in my class and in the classes right above and below mine. For several years, I had been friends with the same five girls: Sheila, Jennifer, Annie, Denise, and Mandy.

We were actually three twosomes who hung out in pairs all day at school and later at home, wore the same clothes, and talked on the phone every night before sleep. The six of us got together as a group on weekends.

This year, though, Annie started dating a boy who went to college in Green Bay, an hour north. She had no time for us on weekends, and even at school, she ate lunch with the few senior girls who had college boyfriends. The day Mandy and I found Denise alone in the cafeteria, we went to sit with her. Like me, Denise was the last kid left on her family's farm, but she was allowed to drive a beat-up Ford, the family's second car. She started picking up me, then Mandy, in the morning on the way to school.

The week before Halloween, the trees, with their few clinging leaves, looked as bedraggled and misshapen as haunted-house monsters. The lawns in town had Halloween displays: jack-o'-lanterns, giant spiders, witches, vampires, scarecrows. Some family had decorated the ornamental cherry tree in front of their house with little spooks made from white handkerchiefs. Each spook, dangling from a string tied around its neck, had a round head stuffed with cloth. My mother and I once made a doll like that to hang in our window in Japan on the night before an outdoor picnic. Called a *teru teru bozu* or sunshine monk, the doll was believed to bring good weather. If rain spoiled our outing, we were supposed to cut off his head and throw him away. The next morning, we woke up to the sound of raindrops hitting the windowpane, but my mother couldn't bring herself to chop off the doll's head. She put him back in the drawer with her scarves. Back then, she was gentle—*yasashii,* we said in

112   Kyoko Mori

Japanese—not tough and strict the way she became after we moved to the farm.

In the car, Denise was talking about something she saw on TV. I didn't interrupt. When I remembered my childhood, I didn't tell my friends, not even Mandy. A long time ago, in grade school, I did. Most of the kids thought I was bragging about having lived somewhere they'd never been, making up stories about the few things I remembered. We'd get into arguments and minor scuffles. Once, I punched Clayton Vander Zanden for calling me a liar, and he punched me back. Both of us ended up with bruises and detention.

My mother was so upset with me she cried, but I didn't care. If people refused to believe me when I was telling the truth, that was their problem, not mine. After we were in middle school, though, the kids who used to call me a liar just rolled their eyes and said nothing when I talked about Japan. My close friends smiled politely but seemed embarrassed by the odd details I recalled about the hilltop apartment where my mother and I had lived, the pink and purple neon signs outside department stores, the sea in the distance with its sharp, salty smell. I was like someone who claimed to have been abducted by a UFO or to have entered a tunnel of light while she lay in a coma. No matter how vivid my memory, to my story just sounded weird to everyone else. So I said nothing about the *teru teru bozu* as Denise and I drove toward Mandy's house.

When Mandy got in the car, wearing my sweatshirt from UW-Stevens Point, Caroline's school, Denise asked, "What are you guys doing for Halloween?"

"We're going to that dance at school," I answered. It was

the only school dance all year we could go to without a date and not feel stupid.

"You can come with us," Mandy added.

"We're going as Tweedledee and Tweedledum," I explained. "We already have our costumes."

"You can be Alice," Mandy offered.

"Yeah, your hair's the right length."

"That's so childish," Denise said. "The dance doesn't start till eight. What are you going to do till then?"

"We're going to get ready at Mandy's house so her sister can take pictures."

"It gets dark at five now." Denise waited.

I didn't know what she was getting at. I looked back over my shoulder at Mandy, who shrugged.

Then Denise asked, "Have you guys ever done a Halloween prank?"

We shook our heads.

"You want to do one before the dance?"

"I don't know. My sister Caroline says putting toilet paper on lawns and trees is bad for the environment, especially if you use colored paper—you're spreading dyes and chemicals."

"Who said I wanted to TP people's yards? We should do something real."

"Like what?" I expected her to suggest moving someone's car to the other side of the street, or writing shaving-cream graffiti on store windows—the sort of things the more serious pranksters, usually boys, did.

"I have a can of black paint from when my brother painted his basement room. It's still good. I already checked."

None of my friends had ever written graffiti on the sidewalk, but maybe it would be okay if we didn't write any obscenities. We could copy the words to our school song, or the "Jabberwocky" poem.

"You know that white picket fence in front of Old Man Hansen's house?" Denise said. "We can paint a good section of it black."

"You're kidding, right?"

Denise took her eyes off the road to give me an icy stare. She was a tall, big-boned girl with pale blue eyes, which she described as "gray" on her driver's license. "No, I'm not kidding. That old man ruined our summer. I hate him."

Mr. Hansen, a retired pharmacist who attended our church, had scolded us for making too much noise by the pool at Annie's house, next door to his. Most afternoons, he came down as soon as we went outside. When he said our music gave him a headache, we turned down our radio, but it was never quiet enough for him. After he spoke to Annie's parents, we had to stop playing any music. Then he said we were bothering him by shrieking and screaming, which we only did when someone managed a back flip off the diving board or a couple of us got into a splashing contest.

One afternoon, when we were perfectly quiet, just sitting on our towels and painting our toenails, he complained that the smoke from Denise's cigarette was drifting into his house. He said his wife had died of lung cancer even though she'd never smoked one single cigarette because of selfish people like us who did. Denise was the only one smoking, but Mr. Hansen yelled at all of us. When our eyes met, he looked away as though he didn't even know me. I had attended his wife's funeral with my family, so I'd been feeling sorry for him, even though I hadn't said anything to my friends. Now I was just as mad at him as everyone else. My friends and I stopped swimming at Annie's. Every time I dove off the public dock into the cold water of a nearby lake and came up with slimy weeds tangled around my neck, I had bad thoughts about Mr. Hansen. Still, I didn't think we should ruin his fence just because we didn't like him.

"Mr. Hansen acted like a jerk," I said, "but Halloween pranks are supposed to be for fun, not revenge. Besides, I don't want to get into trouble."

"You have no guts, Asako," Denise spat out. "I'll go alone. Just don't be a tattletale as well as a coward, okay?"

No one spoke again for several minutes.

"Don't be so upset," Mandy finally said from the backseat. "Of course we won't tell anyone. Who knows—maybe we'll do the prank with you. We'll think about it."

Her voice sounded squeaky and panicked. The hair on the back of my neck stood up. When we drove past that house with the cherry tree again, I pictured all the spooks with their heads chopped off.

Mandy and I stayed after school for our cross-country practice and then started back toward my house. We had to walk, since we had no ride.

"I can't believe you told Denise we were going to consider doing that prank," I said when we were a few blocks away from school.

Mandy stopped on the sidewalk and switched her gym bag

from one shoulder to the other. We had over a mile to go and it was already dark and chilly. "I only said that so Denise wouldn't be mad at us. But the more I think about it, the more I'm tempted."

"You're crazy."

"Mr. Hansen treated us like a bunch of juvenile delinquents. We weren't even that noisy."

"But painting a fence is vandalism. Right now, Mr. Hansen's the only person who thinks we're troublemakers. If we get caught, everyone else will think that about us too. Besides, maybe Mr. Hansen's been so cranky because his wife died. Maybe we should give him the benefit of the doubt."

"Oh, what's the point of being so good, Asako?" Mandy shook her head. "Look at us walking home in the dark like a couple of losers. We go out for cross-country even though our team never wins. Then we have to walk home because our parents are too busy to pick us up. We study hard to go to college when all we can afford is a state school. Our high school's such a joke that we don't even have a French teacher."

We walked into the countryside, careful to stay on the far left side of the gravel road. At my house, Don would be cleaning out the barn and my mother would be cooking dinner. She would make a sour face and get very quiet when Mandy and I told her that we wanted to heat up a frozen pizza and eat in my room while we did our homework. Later she'd make a big deal about letting me drive Mandy back to her house. My mother worried about me crashing into other people's fences or scratching their cars in parking lots. Endlessly, she cautioned me not to cause trouble, on purpose or by accident. If she knew that Denise was planning to paint Mr. Hansen's fence black, she would forbid me to speak to her again.

"We can't talk about this in my house," I said to Mandy. "Not even in my room."

She rolled her eyes. "What do you think I am? Stupid?"

A car was coming down the road. We stepped aside to let it pass. Bits of gravel bounced off the road in the car's wake, and a gust blew a pile of dead leaves into the ditch at our feet. I thought about how Caroline had studied hard and gotten straight A's in her junior and senior years. She didn't complain about only going to a state school. She would never ruin someone's fence and pretend it was a prank. But then again, my mother hadn't nagged and scolded her in spite of her good behavior, treating her like a troublemaker before she even did anything.

"Hey, I'm sick of being a Goody Two-shoes too," I said as we started walking again. "Yeah, I am. What's the point?" I wasn't sure how much I meant that, but the funny thing about saying something pessimistic in the dark, with the leaves falling all around, is that your voice sounds so lonely and bitter. You begin to believe what you're saying, completely. Anyway, Denise was right about one thing: It got plenty dark by five o'clock.

On Halloween, which was on a Saturday, Denise showed up at Mandy's house in a black leather jacket and torn jeans, her hair dyed green. Mandy and I had put on jeans, dark flannel shirts, and navy blue seed company baseball caps my stepfather, Don, had in our garage.

Kyoko Mori

"Why did you do that to your hair?" I asked when I got into the passenger seat.

"I'm in disguise," Denise said, starting the car. "I'm dressed like a punk rocker."

"But the whole idea was for us to be inconspicuous."

"No one thinks I have green hair."

"If someone sees us in Mr. Hansen's neighborhood and then later at the dance, they'll say, oh, it was that kid with green hair. Then everyone will know it was you."

Mandy pulled off her baseball cap and tossed it into the front. "Here," she said. "Asako's right."

"What about you?" Denise asked.

"Let's say I'm less conspicuous than you are. Don't argue. Put the hat on. I'm not going otherwise."

North Holland was fifteen blocks from east to west, with a two-block downtown in the middle. Mr. Hansen lived near the eastern edge, but we parked behind the bank on Main Street. The can of paint, a screwdriver, and the brushes were in a thin plastic bag in the trunk.

"We can't carry them like that," Mandy said. "What if the bag breaks?"

I had brought my black gym bag just in case. I took the paint and the tools from Denise, put them in my bag, and lifted the bag onto my shoulder.

We walked through town without speaking. A few cars drove past us, but we kept our heads down. There were no little kids trick-or-treating; they had gone earlier with their parents. Under the lamplight, the wisps of hair sticking out of Denise's hat shone lime green. I pulled my own hat down farther. It was too late to turn back. If Mandy and Denise got caught alone, Denise would think I'd told on them. She and Mandy would start spending time together without me. In the week I'd had to think it over, I had convinced myself that I was doing everyone a favor by going along. I'd make sure that we caused only a little damage and left without getting caught.

Mr. Hansen's front porch and living room were dark, but his car was in the driveway. The street was deserted. Everyone was probably at dinner, or like Annie, at a Halloween party somewhere; she'd told Sheila that she was going to one with her boyfriend. As we crouched in front of Mr. Hansen's fence, Denise glanced toward Annie's house. Annie was the first in our group to ever have a boyfriend. We were scary smart girls who didn't flirt and giggle; no boy at school wanted to date us. If Mandy started spending all her time with a guy she had just met, I might have wanted to pour paint on someone's fence too. Maybe Denise blamed Mr. Hansen for her best friend's defection—if we'd kept hanging out by Annie's pool all summer, she might have stayed with us instead.

I took out the stuff from my bag. I shook the paint can and popped the lid open with the screwdriver. Then I dipped the brushes and handed them out.

"Here goes nothing," Denise said, sliding her brush down the fence post in front of her. She made a thick, even stroke right in the middle. For a while, Mandy and I just stared.

"Maybe we should paint every other post really black," I

said when Denise looked back at us. "You know, make a design."

"Like a zebra?" Denise smirked.

"Sure," I said, moving to Denise's left, skipping one post, and touching my brush to the second one. Mandy crawled to her right and started on the other side. I pushed the paint can so it was behind Denise and we could all reach it. The paint was thick; we had to reload our brushes after each stroke.

We had each completed our first post and were halfway through the second when the porch light came on. The paint had been drying my eyes out, making me blink a lot. At first, I noticed only that it was suddenly much easier to see and that the paint I thought I was applying evenly actually looked streaked. Then the door opened and Mr. Hansen came out in his long-sleeved shirt and pants, but no coat. "Who's there?" he yelled from the porch. "What's going on?" By the time he started shuffling down the porch steps, about twenty yards from the fence, Denise and Mandy had already dropped their brushes and were on their feet, running. I threw my brush on the sidewalk and started running after them before I remembered my gym bag. I had emptied it that afternoon, so there was nothing inside with my name on it, but how would I explain its loss to my mother or Don? Mr. Hansen was at the bottom of the steps; that gave me a few more seconds. I twisted around, dashed back, and grabbed the bag from the sidewalk. While he was still on the walkway, I turned again and took off. Ahead, Mandy was clearing the corner of the cross street and Denise was right behind her. Her hat had come off, and her green hair trailed behind her like a flag.

Mr. Hansen was wheezing somewhere behind me, but I didn't look back.

I sprinted around the corner and caught up with Denise halfway down the block. She had stopped and was bent over panting, hands on her knees. "Keep running," I said as I sped past her. "Don't be stupid."

I ran all the way back to the parking lot, where Mandy was in the backseat of Denise's car, her head slumped down so no one would see her. I climbed into the passenger seat, shoving the empty gym bag onto the floor.

"We have to go back if she doesn't come in a few minutes," I said.

Mandy nodded.

I pictured Mr. Hansen gaining on Denise and grabbing her by her green hair. When Denise limped into the parking lot alone, I was so relieved that I didn't mind how she berated us all the way back to Mandy's house.

"You track stars left me alone out there," she said. "You couldn't care less what happened to me."

Mandy and I had to put on our costumes and go to the dance, because we'd been telling her family and our friends about it for weeks. We'd gotten identical men's extra-large white pants from a secondhand store and black-and-white striped shirts and white socks from Kmart; we'd dyed our old tennis shoes black and pasted black paper wedges and brims to a couple of white berets to make two-toned bowler hats. While Denise sat on Mandy's bed and read a magazine, we put on the outfits, stuffed round pillows into our pants,

Kyoko Mori

and tied strips of torn white bedsheet around our necks. Mandy's mother and sister exclaimed over our clever costumes and took picture after picture. I had a hard time smiling and looking excited. The stripes on our shirts alternated black, white, black, white, just like those six posts we had painted. Maybe that was what gave me the idea about skipping every other post, even though I thought I was suggesting it to keep our damage small. The shirts screamed out our guilt.

As we drove to school in Denise's car, I pictured Mr. Hansen clutching his chest and falling down on the sidewalk. What if we'd given him a heart attack?

"Hey, we didn't get caught," Denise said when we got out of the car in the school parking lot. "Don't be so glum."

"I can be glum if I want to be," Mandy said. She looked sideways into my face. "And Asako, too," she said.

Sheila and Jennifer were waiting for us at the gym door. Dressed like bees with big antennae on their heads, they shrieked and laughed when they saw Mandy and me. Mandy opened and closed the black umbrella she carried and I shook my rattle, but we did not recite the nursery rhymes we had memorized. We went inside and joined a bunch of girls dressed like nurses, nuns, witches, cats, and Morticia from The Addams Family. Across the gym, boys stood in their own clusters. There were Frankensteins and Draculas, a zombie, an accident victim, and a butcher. The few punk kids gathered in the corner wearing their torn jeans and black leather jackets, but they dressed like that every day, which was why Denise's costume was stupid.

While Mandy went to get a drink of water, I joined a dozen other girls on the dance floor. The DJ, a boy from the senior class, played the Red Hot Chili Peppers. He followed it with a couple of Britney Spears songs, which were mindless but good for dancing. By the time we were jumping up and down with Jennifer Lopez, shouting out "I'm Real," I started feeling a little more optimistic. Mandy had joined another circle of girls. After a couple more songs, our two groups would become one big circle, and the DJ would know enough to keep playing only the fast songs. I decided Mr. Hansen hadn't died of a heart attack and Denise's hat must have come off only after she was out of his sight. He'd probably mistaken us for a bunch of boys. After the usual rowdies were questioned and then exonerated, the crime would remain a mystery. We would tell Sheila and Jennifer the truth then, but only after swearing them to secrecy.

When Mrs. Peterson, our English teacher, came onto the gym floor, I thought she had decided to dance with us. She was dressed all in black like a witch, complete with a cape and a hat, though no broom. The DJ was playing Eminem. I wondered if Mrs. Peterson might even talk about rap music when we got to the poetry unit in our junior English class. Mrs. Peterson was only twenty-five or -six. She often came to school in blue jeans and a turtleneck, her red hair tied back with a scrunchie. Everyone knew that she was by far the coolest, most up-to-date teacher we had. When she tapped my shoulder and tilted her head sideways, I didn't realize she was

Kyoko Mori

pointing to the door. She put her hand on my arm and pulled me toward her gently.

Everyone around me stopped dancing. Even though the music went on, we were suddenly in the middle of the eerie silence that falls on a crowd when someone's in trouble. That someone was me, though I didn't realize it until I'd followed Mrs. Peterson out of the gym into the hallway, where Officer Daniels, one of the two policemen in our town, was waiting. With kids standing behind him in the doorway dressed like a cowboy, an Indian, and a sheriff, his uniform looked like a costume.

"Follow me," Officer Daniels said.

We went into the classroom where our cross-country team sometimes had meetings. Mr. Hansen was already sitting there, this time wearing a blue nylon jacket a lot like my stepfather Don's. The room only had those school chairs with the tiny writing surface attached to the arm, and even though he was a skinny man, Mr. Hansen looked too big, like a crumpled marionette, in the chair. He shook his head when he saw me come in.

"I never thought you would do something so disrespectful," he said.

"You know what this is about," Officer Daniels said to me.

Mr. Hansen's face wasn't red like when he came to yell at us. It was ash-colored, and his mouth was set hard. "I saw you," he said. "You wrecked my fence and ran away." He must have been much closer to me than I'd thought when I'd gone back for my bag.

I hadn't been able to wash off all the black paint caught under my fingernails. I closed my hands into fists even though it was too late.

"Asako, you should say something." Mrs. Peterson put her hand on my shoulder. She had taken off her witch hat and cape and placed them on an empty chair.

I laid Tweedledum's rattle on the chair next to her things. "Yeah, it was me," I said.

"Who else?" the officer asked. We were standing in the doorway. No one had asked me to sit down.

"I can't tell you."

Mrs. Peterson said nothing even though she knew that Mandy was my best friend. When she handed out grammar worksheets and reading quizzes, she gave Mandy, me, and one other girl library passes to go and read on our own.

"You know we can find out," Officer Daniels said.

"Then why don't you."

"Oh, Asako." Mrs. Peterson sighed.

"I can go back to the gym and ask over the loudspeaker who came to the dance with you."

"How do you know it was the people I came to the dance with? It's been hours since we did the prank."

"So you weren't alone."

"No," I had to admit.

"How many others?"

"I can't say."

"Mr. Hansen saw three paintbrushes. Isn't that right?"

The old man nodded. I shrugged. Maybe I could have gone on like that for hours. I didn't think Officer Daniels would really go up to the DJ's microphone and ask a bunch of kids at a dance to help him solve a crime. But after I shook my head for a couple more minutes, we heard footsteps in the hallway. Mandy ran into the room, with Denise a few

Kyoko Mori

steps behind her. Our identical costumes gave away everything. Mandy hugged me and the two of us started crying. Mrs. Peterson put her arms around us, and drew Denise close too.

When our parents arrived, Mr. Hansen told us that he didn't intend to drag us to the police station and press charges. He was going to have those fence posts replaced, though, and he fully expected us, or our parents, to pay.

"It was just a prank," Denise said, but her mother yanked her by the arm and shushed her. Mr. Hansen got up from his chair and left while Denise and her mother were arguing. The stiff way he walked out of the room showed what he thought of us: We were such scum he didn't even want to demand or hear our apology.

Don drove while my mother sat sideways in the passenger seat, glaring at me but saying nothing. She was the queen of the silent treatment. She knew how to make you squirm until you were almost glad to be yelled at. She seldom scolded me in front of Don, who wasn't as strict. This time, though, he would have nothing to say in my defense. I had disappointed them both. Until that night, they'd only come to school to talk to our teachers at parent-teacher conferences. Caroline had never done anything to hurt other people. When she thought someone had been unfair to her, she talked to the person out in the open. Tracy once got detention for being in a food fight in the cafeteria, but she was only in seventh grade then.

My mother waited till we were home, followed me into my

room, and shut the door. She hadn't taken off her brown jacket, and underneath she was wearing a straight gray skirt and a blue sweater, the clothes she wore to church. I was still dressed like Tweedledum; the pillow had come out, and I had to hold my pants with my hands to make them stay up.

"Sit down," she said, pointing to my desk chair. With her hair pulled back into a bun, her eyes had a scary, tight look. She had high cheekbones and a little nose, just like mine, but there were wrinkles between her eyes and around her mouth. "I asked Don not to go with me," she said when I sat down. She hadn't moved from the doorway. "I wanted to spare him the embarrassment, but he insisted."

I said nothing.

"He went with me so he could show those people you and I are his family even though we are foreigners."

"I'm sick of you saying we're foreigners," I blurted out. "I know what I did was wrong. But I'm not a foreigner. Denise and Mandy did the same thing. I'm sure their parents are just as embarrassed."

"You understand nothing," my mother hissed. "How do you think Mr. Hansen knew it was you? Officer Daniels said you were the only one he recognized."

"I was the last to get away. He knows me from church."

"No." She shook her head hard. "He saw you because you were so easy to spot. You look like no one else."

"We looked the same in the dark," I said, but my voice sounded shaky.

"Maybe he didn't even have to see," my mother said. "He knew it had to be the foreign girl."

"That's a terrible thing to say."

Kyoko Mori

"You know nothing." With that, my mother slammed the door and walked out.

The next day I skipped church, though my mother had said I was grounded indefinitely except for going to church and school; I wasn't even supposed to use the phone. After I heard the truck drive away, I put on my running clothes and shoes. I wanted to call Mandy, but her parents wouldn't let her answer the phone. If I called Caroline, maybe no one would notice when the phone bill came, because Don called her often too, but I didn't want to tell her about the terrible and stupid thing I'd done. I ran to the marsh instead and followed the gravel trail, and when I came to the place where there was a big rock Caroline and I used to sit on, I stopped.

If I ran straight through, I could get home before my mother and Don returned from church. It seemed pointless, though, to try to avoid trouble when I was already grounded indefinitely. How could something be more indefinite than "indefinite"? If the universe was infinite, what was on the other side of it? That was the kind of question I wrote about in my journal for Mrs. Peterson's class. "You're one of the best writers I've ever taught," she'd told me. "I hope you'll pursue your writing when you go to college." After what happened last night, she might think of me only as the selfish girl who did mean things to old people. Or the foreigner who was up to no good. Maybe Mrs. Peterson had been impressed with my writing in the first place only because I wrote well for someone born in another country.

The air was dry but cold. I began to shiver. "You speak such good English," people said to my mother at church gatherings and town picnics. My mother always nodded politely, but inside she was fuming. On the drive home, she'd say, "I've been speaking English longer than that man's been alive. Why does he assume I don't know how to talk?" My mother had taken English lessons in Japan, which was why she was able to give Don directions when he got lost in Kobe, and why they fell in love. By the time she came to Wisconsin, she could speak like anyone else.

"Will you be going home to Japan this summer?" Mr. Waters at the general store asked us every May.

"That's not my home anymore," my mother would answer.

"You must have some family left there," he'd say, not catching her tone.

Because she didn't want to explain that her family refused to see or hear from her after she left my father to marry an American, my mother would reply, "Anyway, Don and I are too busy at the farm to travel."

When I was new at our school, kids wanted to know if my mother and I had lived in paper houses, if my mother had been a geisha, if we ate raw fish every day. But that was a long time ago. I'd figured that my friends had gotten to know me as me: Asako who was a cross-country runner, a good writer, a scary smart girl. But maybe they had just run out of dumb questions to ask.

A flock of white-throated sparrows had landed several yards ahead of me. They were pecking at the grass, foraging among the fallen leaves. Some had white stripes on their heads and on others the stripes were off-white, almost tan, but every

Kyoko Mori

bird had a yellow dot above a pink bill, a white patch on the throat, and a clear gray breast. Anyone, and not just a bird-watcher, could tell that they were all the same type of bird.

Even when I was dressed in my flannel shirt and jeans, or in that stupid Tweedledum costume next to Mandy's Tweedledee, I had never blended in. If these sparrows were like the other girls at school, then I was something altogether different—more like the escaped parakeet Caroline and I once spotted in a flock of starlings. The parakeet, a mimic like the starlings, thought he had found his flock. But his green feathers made him conspicuous even in the sky. It was October or November when we saw that bird. He was doomed to freeze to death in a couple of months, while the starlings, hardy birds, would manage to winter over without migrating south.

My legs were beginning to cramp. Soon, it would be too late to get up and run home, but I didn't care.

"I knew you were here," Caroline said when she came down the path toward me in her jeans and denim jacket. Her long blond hair was tied back in a ponytail. I didn't know it was her until she was thirty steps away. "Your running shoes and jacket were gone, so I knew you weren't at church."

"What are you doing here?"

"I came to see *you*," she said, sitting down next to me. "No one was home when I stopped by. I left a note saying that I insisted on taking you out."

"What did you do that for?"

"What kind of greeting is that?" She put her arms around me. "Give me a hug, kiddo."

I leaned sideways into her hug and squeezed her shoulder.

"You know they can't ground *me*," she said.

"How do you know I was grounded?"

"Dad told me on the phone. He said you were in trouble."

"Don asked you to come home?"

"No. We were just having our Sunday morning chat."

"He told you what I did."

She nodded. Her eyes widened a little. "It probably wasn't your idea," she offered.

"No, but that's no excuse. I know I did a terrible thing." I wanted to tell her that I wasn't out here because of the vandalism but because of what my mother had said. But if my mother was right, then it was no use talking to Caroline: No matter how much I looked up to her, she would never be my sister. My mother and I were foreigners to everyone, even to our own family.

"I bet it wasn't as bad as you think," Caroline said. "I'm sure you had to run away before you were able to do much damage."

"We each painted two fence posts. Maybe some paint got on the others, too."

"Dad said the restitution isn't going to be so bad. You can work it off by helping him with the haying next summer."

I thought of the heat, the little pieces of grass getting under my shirt.

"I'll come and do half your share if they let me. Anyway, Dad said the damage wasn't very serious, but your mother was very upset."

Kyoko Mori

"I don't want to talk about it."

"Okay." She shrugged. "You're getting cold. We should go."

I followed her to her car, an old Subaru station wagon. "I don't want to go home."

"We'll drive into town and get something to eat," she said. "I didn't have breakfast yet. I'll tell your mother it was my idea, I dragged you. We'll go to Marge's."

Marge's Diner would be crowded with families after church. Everyone would look up from their plate and see me, a juvenile delinquent and a foreigner.

"I don't want to go unless I can sit in the car and wait. You have to get the food to go."

"All right," she said. "Whatever you say."

The first four-way stop in town was a few blocks from Mr. Hansen's house. Caroline came to a full stop even though no car was oncoming. "So I was wondering," she said. "Do you mind if I see the fence?"

"Oh, come on. What for?"

"I'm wondering if Dad's right. He and your mother seemed to disagree, but neither of them actually saw what you did."

I remembered the grainy, streaky lines I'd made with my brush. My stomach felt queasy. But Caroline was already turning the car.

"I'm curious," she said. "I know you'll never again do anything like this. So I've got to see your one and only hard-core prank."

She slowed down when we came to Mr. Hansen's block. I'd half imagined a crowd gawking at the fence, but no one was there. Mr. Hansen's fence stretched in front and around the side of his house; the twelve-post section we'd painted, in the corner, was only a small part of it. Black, white, black, white, black, white it went, for maybe six feet. The posts didn't look like zebra stripes at all.

One morning in early spring when I was about six, I saw a crowd gathered in front of someone's house down the hill from our apartment in Kobe. A large flower wreath hung on the front door, but even I could tell that these were not flowers for happiness. White chrysanthemums and dark green cedars were wrapped in black and white ribbons, and all around the house, black and white drapes were tacked onto the siding, making the house look like a strange tent. The men and women who stood on the sidewalk were dressed in black.

"It's a funeral," my mother had said, quickening her steps and pulling me along. "It's bad luck to watch."

But both that time and the few other times I saw the same black and white ribbons and drapes, I could not help but stare at the people who stood in front like a huge gathering of crows.

I had painted Mr. Hansen's fence with funeral colors, making his house look like a mockery of a house in mourning. Mrs. Hansen's funeral had been in the spring, on a cold and rainy afternoon. The couple's son, who spoke at the service, said his parents had been planning a fifty-year anniversary in the fall. "Mom wanted to live long enough to see that day, but it doesn't matter. My dad and I will always love her."

Kyoko Mori

Mr. Hansen hugged his son and they both cried. Alone among my friends, I had seen his tears, and yet I said nothing to my friends a few months later when Mr. Hansen wanted us to be quiet. I didn't try to stop Denise. All I cared about was not getting into trouble.

Caroline had pulled over to the curb in front of his house. Mr. Hansen's car was in the driveway, so we knew he had gotten back from church, if he'd gone at all. If I were him, I'd probably have stayed home, too angry or sad to face me or my family.

"You can wait here," I said to Caroline.

By the way she put her hand on my shoulder, I knew she understood. All along, this was what she had been hoping for. She hadn't wanted to see the fence—that was an excuse to get me in front of the house. If I saw what I'd done, she must have figured, I would come to my senses and go apologize instead of feeling sorry for myself. Caroline thought the best of me, as she did of most other people; Don did too. My mother didn't, but she had her reasons. She felt beaten down, hopeless, and alone. The dumb comments people made, though not *meant* to offend, rankled inside her, causing her to think the worst of everyone.

It would take me a long time to understand or overcome her bitterness. Every time people made comments about my English, I too would cringe. My face in the mirror would always remind me of how different I looked from my friends, how far away from each other we'd started out. No matter where I lived, I would not be able to take my belonging for granted and automatically trust in people's goodwill, as Caroline could.

But that had nothing to do with the cruel thing I'd done to Mr. Hansen. Whether he recognized me because he knew me from church or because I looked like no one else or both, I owed him an apology.

I walked past the funeral-colored fence posts, up to the porch. I rang the bell and waited until Mr. Hansen opened the door and stepped back to let me in.

HEARING Flower

by M. E. Kerr

"Come," he said when he came off the soccer field. "My older sister wants to meet you. I think she wants to apologize."

"She should after what she called me."

He threw his head back and laughed. "Maybe you heard right the first time. Maybe you *are* a flower face. A rose face. A gardenia face."

But what she had said to him, after the last soccer game I went to—just to watch him—what she had said was "Is that your flour face?"

I heard "flower."

I didn't hear the next wisecrack, but Esteban told me.

She'd said, "The Santiagos don't want any white babies running around, Esteban."

I tried to be cool when he told me his sister had said that. I smiled down at his brown eyes and said, "She's rushing things, isn't she?"

"Because she knows I like you . . . that way."

See, I don't care anymore that he's short. I've fallen in love for the first time, I tell my diary, and my diary can't roll its eyes to the heavens and say, "What about Christopher Bennett?"

That was a whole year ago. I was only fifteen then.

Chris cannot hold a candle to Esteban Santiago.

Can you picture Christopher Bennett strolling out on the small stage at The Coffeehouse, grinning and bowing and then singing until his eyes are shining like stars, his face wet with sweat and the crowd going crazy calling out his name? That's what happens every night since Esteban started working there.

As we got to the battered old red Toyota where Gioconda Santiago sucked on a cigarette and waited to pass judgment on me, Esteban whispered, "Don't let her intimidate you." Then in a proud tone he said to her, "Gioconda, meet Bianca Brown."

"I've been waiting to meet you," she said to me. "Last time, after the game, you ran away."

"I didn't know you wanted to meet me," I said. I felt like saying, "If I'm such a flour face why are you interested?"

Gioconda said, "You see my *virgencita* here?" She used her cigarette to point at a plastic statue of the Virgin Mary on the dashboard. One of those plastic nodding dogs was next to it.

"Yes, I see."

"I pray to it," she said.

"Well, good. Good." I was embarrassed. We Browns pray, but we don't talk about it.

"I drive along praying," said Esteban's sister.

I couldn't think of anything to say to that, and it turned

M. E. Kerr

out I didn't have to answer, because her next sentence came rolling off her tongue, with a mean smile that made her eyes crinkle. "I pray that Esteban will tell you to stop chasing after him!"

"Come on, Bianca!" Esteban said. "Let's get out of here. When will I learn that I cannot trust her to behave? I am sorry. I did not know she would do that!"

His sister was not finished. She shouted over her shoulder, "Stop throwing yourself at my brother, Flour Face. He laughs behind your back!"

"*Do* you laugh behind my back?" I asked him.

"I do not, Bianca."

"What's the *matter* with her, Esteban?"

"She takes my mother's place now that we came here. My mother is back in Nicaragua, so my sister thinks she has to keep an eye on me."

"What does she think you're going to do?"

"She is more concerned with what *you* are going to do. Maybe you will take me away from my family, from my country. Do you think you will do that?" He laughed. He had a nice laugh. His eyes crinkled too. He was so great-looking. I didn't care that he was short. That never bothered Nicole Kidman when she was with Tom Cruise.

"I have something to tell you," Esteban said. He took my hand as we walked along."I am going to do some work for your father."

"*WHAT?*"

"Friday afternoon I'm going to put the new roof on your garage. Dario Lopez from our house was supposed to do it, but he has to take a driver's test to get his license."

"Since when are you a carpenter, Esteban?"

"Since I said I would do it."

The Latinos in our town are my father's new work crew. They work for five dollars an hour.

"For them, it's a good deal," my father says defensively. "Most of them don't speak English, and some don't even have papers. I give them steady work. They learn on the job. They can make as much as three hundred a week."

My brother was after him all summer, saying things like "You call yourself a contractor? You hire slave laborers, Dad. And you haven't hired any real local workers in years!"

"You college boys don't know zilch about the working world," said Kenneth Brown to Kenyon Brown. "The only thing you really know how to do is spend money someone else earns."

"I've been waiting tables all summer, Dad, in case you don't remember."

"Oh, is that a job? Do you have any calluses? Is your neck sunburned? If you want to know what work is, watch these Latinos. They're a whole new breed, Kenyon! We've never had people like them. They sock away three quarters of what they earn. They send it to their families."

"So did the Irish when they used to come here summers."

"The Irish never stuck around more than a few months. These people buy houses."

"One house for twenty people. They group."

"There's a housing shortage now," my father snapped, "but the town will rectify it. Why can't people accept change?

They're the best thing that ever happened out here."

"Out here" is the tip of Long Island, the Hamptons. We are a resort town in the summer, but more and more people are staying with us longer, and more vacationers are buying their homes. We are growing fast, and the new immigrants are part of the picture.

They come from everywhere: Mexico, Colombia, Costa Rica, Brazil, Cuba. They have changed a lot of things about this town. In the supermarkets now there are green plantains, yuca, calabaza, and batata. Many church sermon boards are in Spanish and English, and there are small delis popping up which sell paella, arroz con pollo, quesadillas, burritos, and tamales.

The biggest dilemma they have posed is finding a place to build their sports fields. They are soccer players; they all seem to be. Nobody wants the fields in his backyard. Last summer my father was the only man in our neighborhood who spoke up for the fields when they wanted to put them a few blocks from our house. The vote went against the soccer players, and now the town is clearing land by the dump for them.

"What is the matter with people?" my father said. "We have our golf courses and our tennis courts, our baseball diamonds and our football fields. But we just can't take the idea of good clean fun going on in our neighborhoods if the sport is soccer. We all know who the soccer players are."

"That's not why," my brother would argue. "Don't make a race thing out of it. People don't want the noise in their backyards. They don't want the lights at night. They don't want the public rest rooms."

"People should be glad the muchachos want to recreate in their spare time," said Dad. "You don't see *them* crawling in windows to rob, or hanging around the parking lots to smoke dope and key cars."

There was a fair chance that my father would like Esteban. He admires hard workers, since he is one himself. He did not take to Christopher Bennett. Summers, all Christopher did was surf and sail, because his family was rich. But Christopher's big faux pas was to honk the horn for me the night of our first date. Dad made me sit in the living room until Christopher figured out he had to knock on our front door and come in our house to meet my father before I went anywhere with him. Dad also thoroughly examined Christopher's driving license.

Our garage hasn't had a car in it for years. My father fixed the space up for my brother, a private room of his own because it was something Dad had never had when he was a kid; he'd shared a bed with his three brothers in a two-bedroom house.

Now, with Kenyon in his senior year at college, Dad was reclaiming that part of our house. Kenyon planned to go to New York and get a job in advertising. Of all things, Dad was creating a screening room. It was part of his plan to begin dating again, or as he put it, "to find the right woman for my old age." He said he knew he would never find someone like our mother. He used to say Mom was his university, that she had taught him "culture," that he had not had an original thought in his head for twenty-five years until he married her.

He would tell Kenyon and me that he had wanted to name his son Kenneth Brown Jr. and me Mary Brown after his grandma. But my mother had taught him how important names were, and that if you had an ordinary last name, you deserved an exotic first name. Over my Mom's desk was a sampler she'd made which said: MY HEART IS FREE, MY HEAD UNBOWED, I DO NOT JOIN THE FOOLISH CROWD.

My father had gotten a crew together to install a hardwood floor and new windows with shutters in the garage. He had gotten a permit for a shower, a stove, and a sink. He bought a wide-screen TV and a projector. Then came all new furniture. Two leather chairs that reclined, a leather couch that could convert to a bed. Thick rugs. Fancy recessed lighting. A white marbletop coffee table that swiveled up to a full-size dining table. My father had learned a lot working for the movie moguls and investment bankers who flocked to our shores summers and weekends. This "spare room" didn't look like any other room in our little house.

"Esteban Santiago told me he's going to do The Screening Room roof Friday afternoon," I said to Dad at dinner that night.

"How did you know I hired him, and how do you know him?" Dad asked.

"He's a senior, so I see him around school. And I've heard him sing at The Coffeehouse. He's fabulous!"

"Do you see him on a regular basis?"

"I watch soccer, and he plays."

"You watch soccer?"

"Sometimes." I should have said I do when Esteban plays, but I didn't know how to tell my father I might be in love with someone I've never really been alone with for more than twenty minutes. . . . All right. Leave out the "love" part. Call it a crush. That makes less of my feelings, but Dad can live with a crush. Mention love and Dad gets that lost look in his eyes that says he wishes Mom were alive. Mom would know how to get me through it, or over it, or whatever it takes to get me back on track without any damage being done.

"So this muchacho sings, and he plays soccer, and now he's going to become a carpenter?" said my father.

"Don't call him a 'muchacho,' Dad."

"Why not?" When Dad didn't wait for my answer, I was just as glad. It was too hard to explain to my father that calling Esteban a muchacho was somehow belittling. Dad didn't get that sort of thing. He called women "gals," and Asians "Orientals." Once I heard him talking to a new Latino crew and at the end of his spiel, he said, "So there you are, cha-cha-cha."

Dad said "Santiago is a runt, but he's got good muscles. He can finish that roof in an afternoon. I'm having a little lunch and matinee the next day for a lady friend. I want to impress her. I'm making my spaghetti and she's bringing the movie. I told her I like everything, so when you meet her, don't tell her I only watch war pictures and westerns!"

"Who is this mystery lady?"

"Her name is Larkin."

"Larkin what?"

"Just Larkin. She's an artist. She only uses one name. . . . You should see *her* place."

"Why? What's it like?"

"It looks like something out of a magazine, and I don't mean *Family Circle*. This lady has class, Bianca! I'm not talking about money, either. I'm talking about what your mother was always talking about: originality. I see things a whole new way now. She's taught me how to be chic."

"Dad? That's pronounced 'sheek,' not 'chick'!"

I didn't have to wait until Friday afternoon to see Esteban again. My best friend was entertaining her cousin that Wednesday night, and she chose The Coffeehouse as the place to go after dinner. She invited me along, so that made three girls giggling and poking each other's sides in the front row.

When he finished his set, Esteban jumped down from the stage and asked if I'd sit with him at a table for two and let him buy me a cappuccino.

We could hardly meet each other's eyes, and we were smiling at nothing. We sat so close, too, our arms touching, his small hands caressing the spoon from my coffee. I felt as though we were wired, as though it was electricity we were breathing out, as though we could catch on fire any second. When I looked across at my girlfriend's table, she and her cousin were staring at us. My girlfriend was making faces, trying to ask, "What's going on? Since when do you know *him*?"

When Kenyon called home Thursday night, Dad was at the Unitarian church with Larkin. Dad had told me he was thinking of leaving the Presbyterian church and becoming a Unitarian because their thinking was freer.

Dad had said, "Larkin has given me new eyes. Just for example, Bianca, I never looked at trees before. I never looked at the ocean—I mean *really* looked."

On the phone, I told Kenyon about Esteban. I was sure by

then that Esteban felt the same way I did.

"You haven't even kissed or anything?" Kenyon asked.

"Nothing. But we might as well have. Kenyon? I'd pack my bags and run away with him if he asked me. I wouldn't think a minute."

"Well, if he asks, you ask *him* where he plans to take you—and if he plans to take you to Nicaragua, you'd better think a lot longer than a minute."

"Maybe I'd like Nicaragua. Dad says we all need to open our minds to new things."

"Sure we do, cha-cha-cha," said Kenyon.

I loved the way Esteban looked that Friday. He had a brown-and-white checked bandanna around his forehead, which matched his light brown eyes. His skin was smooth and tan, but you could see where his mustache would be if he hadn't shaved, and his teeth were white, with one on the upper right side slightly crooked. I saw a lot of his teeth, because he couldn't stop smiling. I couldn't either.

My father had a job over in Sag Harbor, so he was hurrying, but he was not in so big a hurry that he didn't say to me, "Bianca, Esteban doesn't need you around while he works. . . . I'm having dinner with Larkin, so don't cook for me."

As soon as he backed out of the driveway, Esteban came down the ladder and said, "You hear him? He won't be around for dinner. I will be, if you want to have a special paella. Bianca, don't touch me yet. Stay away from me, and I will tell you why."

"Why?"

"I want to do this job well. I am proud of what I do. I do

not want a distraction, which is what you are, because you have such soft eyes I ache. Your father will be gone for dinner. I have an uncle who cooks in the Pantigo Deli. He makes the best paella. If you take the bus there for some, you can bring it back here and we will feast when I am finished."

"In The Screening Room!" I said. "We can watch a movie!"

"Oh, yes! I like that idea! I feel good with you, Bianca."

"I do too, with you."

It was hours before I heard him at the door. I told him to come on in. I had decided to make a chocolate cake for dessert. I was wiping my hands on a dish towel I'd tucked into my jeans as an apron when he came up behind me.

We couldn't help ourselves. We were hanging on each other and kissing, but Esteban slammed his fist down on the kitchen table and said, "*Basta!* It is almost dark. I only have a little more to do. I need more nails, so I will run into town and you come along and get the paella. Then we will be all set for a party after work."

Before he went next door to get the nails, Esteban introduced me to his uncle at the deli, and told him to give us extra mussels for the paella.

A voice said, "She doesn't need extra mussels, Esteban—she's muscled her way in pretty good, hah?"

It was Gioconda, of course, with her mean mouth and her crinkly eyes.

What was said next was in Spanish, and was angry, both pairs of Santiago eyes flashing. Gioconda pointed at me, her long nails blood red daggers. Esteban made a fist and held it up to her face as though he would slap her, but she didn't flinch; she knew Esteban would never hit a woman. She marched out the door and he stomped after her, calling over his shoulder to his uncle to make two good paella plates to go.

"Slow down, Esteban," I said as we drove back. His old sixties Pontiac kicked up dust along the highway.

"I am sorry you have to see me so angry, sweetheart," he said. "Gioconda makes me undignified, because she thinks she can boss my life." All I really heard was "sweetheart." A first. I watched him in profile. I thought of a song he had sung right to me at The Coffeehouse: "*Is our romance to continue? Will it be my luck to win you?*"

"I don't care if you're undignified," I said.

"But I care. In my life at this time, I have only my pride and my dignity. They are everything."

"Done!" Esteban said.

I put the outside lights on so we could see, but it was already too dark.

"It is just a roof, I guess," said Esteban. "Nothing much to see. It was not hard. You know, Bianca, if I become a carpenter, I will have real money for a change."

I felt like saying not if you work for my father.

But he wouldn't have to work for him long. He could go into business for himself, eventually.

"Don't you want to be a singer, though, Esteban?"

"Someday. But that is a dream. And at The Coffeehouse I

work for tips. A lot of your people out here don't tip at all—did you know that?"

I made Esteban lie down on the leather couch while I got our dinner ready. I swiveled the table up and put a cloth on it with a candle in a star-shaped holder that Dad had recently bought at Pier 1. I picked our best dishes, white ones with gold stars in the middle. Mom had found them on eBay. We hardly ever used them. But I noticed Dad had moved them from the house to The Screening Room. I had warmed the food and poured cold green tea into tall clear glasses, remembering Dad's new notion (or Larkin's) that you should always be able to see the color of your drink. He'd announced that he would never again drink his nightly scotch-on-the-rocks in a red glass, then put all of our colored glasses in a box for the yard sale he said we'd have one day.

I called Esteban's name, but he had fallen asleep. I went over and tickled his face with the corner of a cloth napkin. ("No more paper napkins" was another rule Dad had created since he'd started hanging out with Larkin.) Esteban didn't budge.

"Hey, you," I said softly, and gently crawled on top of him. "Dinner's ready, sweet man," I cooed. I felt his arms around me. He was blinking and grimacing.

"Sweetheart?" he said. "Turn off the overhead light, please."

"Yes, and I want to light candles for us too."

I was looking for matches when I heard Esteban exclaim, "Oh, no! No!"

Esteban was sitting there staring up at the ceiling.

There were rows and rows of nails coming through the wood on the inside.

It took him a little while to say, "I was mad at Gioconda when I went into the hardware store. I got the wrong-size nails. Oh, Bianca! I have made a terrible mess! How can I ever face your father?"

Saturday morning.

"Larkin?" I said as she stood in the doorway. "Are you Larkin?" I had almost mistaken her for Esteban, her hair was so short.

"You must be Bianca."

"Come in. My father should be right back."

"I'm sure he said to come at noon."

"Something came up he had to attend to."

Dad was a wreck. He had come in late last night, so he had not seen the ceiling until this morning. I'd told him that Esteban had left without eating the paella we were going to share, that he was too ashamed of what he'd done. Esteban had said he would never live it down. He had said that my father would look at his face and then in his mind's eye see nails coming through the ceiling. Right behind the brown of Esteban's eyes were tears. Now he would not even answer his phone.

My father has a unique way of showing how angry he is when he is *really* angry. He gets quiet. He speaks in a low tone. He even gives you these quick little smiles as he says things like, "I told him how important this job was! How could he be so sloppy?" Next he had said, "I'm going down

M. E. Kerr

to that house where they all live. If he calls while I'm gone, tell him to get his tail over here immediately."

"I don't mind that your father's late," Larkin said. She looked at a large silver watch on her wrist, shrugged, and smiled. I liked her looks. You'd turn around on the street if you passed her, to get another glimpse. Short cropped hair, a small, slightly crooked nose. She had on some kind of cape, black silk pants, very high silver heels, and a silver blouse. There was a red-and-silver scarf around her neck.

"Would you like a drink? I'm sure my father will be right back."

"Oh thank you, no. Not in the daytime." So much for the bottle of French champagne my father had put in the refrigerator a week ago.

Larkin handed me a tape. *Backstage at the Kirov.* "This is a documentary about Saint Petersburg's Kirov Ballet. I'm a balletomane. And your father tells me he is too."

"Whatever," I said. I was trying to stop myself from saying that all the time, but the idea of Dad saying he was a "balletomane" boggled my mind. I'd never heard the word before, but I could surmise its meaning. Ballet? My father?

"Are you going to join us for lunch?" Larkin asked.

"Oh no. I think my boyfriend, Esteban, is coming by soon. I hope so, anyway. He has business with my father."

Before Dad had slammed out the door, he had predicted that Esteban would run. That's what "they" did when they made mistakes, he had said, adding, "I don't blame him. What's he going to come back here for? To get hell from me?

To hear me tell him he's not getting one cent until he repairs the damage?"

I'd said, "Maybe he'll come because of me."

"Why because of you?" Then he got it. He just shook his head as though he felt really sorry for me. "Honey, these muchachos—excuse me, these *boys*—aren't anything like your Christopher Bennett. They don't have to answer to anyone."

"Don't scare him, Daddy. I'd like to see him again."

"So would I!" my father had said. "So would I like to see him again!"

"I'll just stroll about and look this place over," Larkin said. "Did your father design it?"

"Most of it," I said.

What was Dad planning to do about lunch? He was so rattled he hadn't made his famous spaghetti sauce, and I didn't see any being defrosted.

Larkin had this great scent about her. A perfume so subtle you only smelled it as she moved around the room. It was like the smoky smell of burning leaves.

"You know what impresses me?" Larkin asked.

"The table?" My father had paid a fortune for that table.

"The ceiling," she said. "It's a very emotional ceiling, very original."

"The *ceiling* impresses you?"

"With its splash of nails, up there in the corner. Whose brilliant idea was that?"

"That," I said, "was the idea of Esteban Santiago."

"The same Esteban who has business with your father?"

I nodded. I almost told her then that what she thought was "emotional" was actually a mistake. But I wanted to watch my father's face when she told him what she thought of it.

"Very daring," she said. She was looking up at it as though it was the Sistine Chapel, which my mom and I had seen in Rome the summer before she died. The famous artist Michelangelo had painted it.

Larkin said, "Kenny told me that he liked working with Latinos. Now I know why."

"Do you like paella?" I asked her.

"Very much."

"We have some from the Pantigo Deli."

"That is the very best deli out here," said Larkin.

"Esteban Santiago's uncle is the cook there."

"You say his name a lot," she said. "It's a lovely name too. Esteban Santiago."

Suddenly my father banged through the door, shouting, "Where is he? Is he here?"

"No hello for me, Kenny?" Larkin said.

"I'm sorry. Of course I have a hello for you."

Dad went across the room to Larkin and hugged her and kissed her. Then he sighed and shook his head and said, "That's some ceiling, huh?"

"It is like you—smooth, but with a small nail salad on the side." Larkin chuckled. "That's what I like about you, Kenny. Although you're not an artist yourself, not necessarily a creative person, you don't stand in the way of originality, do you?"

My father was pondering the question, standing there in

his work clothes, a little grubby, needing a shave. He was looking from the ceiling to Larkin's face. He was trying to figure it out, just beginning to get the drift.

Suddenly I heard the sound of Esteban's old Pontiac rattling up our driveway.

He came.

by Marina Budhos

All the time I ask my mother about my grandparents, but she doesn't answer. "Leave that alone, Jemma," she'll say. "Look at what's in front of you, not behind."

But it doesn't work that easy for me. I'm from Trinidad, Port of Spain, on the high mountain side, where the water runs fast and hard during the rainy season, making the stones bang against our zinc roof. My mom, she brought me to Irvington, New Jersey, seven years ago, when I was eight. She wanted to be a nurse, but instead she works as a nanny for the Silers, who live a couple towns over, in Maplewood, taking care of Tyler, their little boy, and Zoe, the baby.

I feel the people from Trinidad walking beside me all the time, like spirits. I once saw my grandfather, swinging a cutlass as he walked down the road so the tall grass shivered as he passed. He was a bad man, my mother would tell me, and I thought maybe it had something to do with the way he whistled with his mouth tilted to the sky, as if he could talk to God himself. One day he took a boat to Aruba and never came back, leaving Grandma Ida alone with five little children. Grandma Ida, though, she's a cheerful lady. She sings church songs all the time, and the sound comes up full and deep from her chest until everyone, in all the neighboring yards, turns to look and says, "Ida, why you have to show off so much? You think God likes you better because you're loud?"

But it's Grandma Rupa I often think about, my daddy's mother. She was an Indian lady and ran a shop that sold saris and brooms made of coconut husks. When I was little, I liked that place. Everywhere hung fabrics of all kinds of colors, and shiny glittery threads in swirly patterns and soft scarves that wrap full around your shoulders. Grandma Rupa would press her thumb to my forehead and rub my scalp with coconut oil, and then she'd show me how to flip the roti dough on a hot griddle in the back of her store. I don't remember a lot of my grandmother, because my daddy died of cancer that ate away his brain, and we left soon after for America.

I do remember the smell of Grandma Rupa—sharp and dusky-like—and how her scarf would slip around her shoulders and bunch up against my mouth. She showed me her little gods—Lakshmi, the pretty one who would make her money, was her favorite—and once, for Divali, she gave me a velvet bag filled with gold bangles and earrings with little ruby chips. "Save those," my mother told me. "That way everyone will know you've got Indian blood too. You're a princess with a dowry, straight from India."

When I walk through the halls of Irvington High, no one knows I've got Indian blood. Sometimes when I look in the mirror I can see my grandmother's face: I see her eyebrows, like two black feathers, meeting over my eyes. And my nose is long and sharp, and I have wrists so small the bangles, they slip right off, so I never wear them. They know something is different about me, though. "You stuck-up," the girls who hang out by the front doors always say to me when I walk past. They pull at my hair, which is straight black, with a little kink in it, and swings at my back. Mama told me don't pay them no mind. She's light-skinned, caramel-colored with brown freckles, and in the summer her curls turn red. In Trinidad we don't think anything of people being mixed, but ever since we come up here, it's different.

"Hey, you!" Jared calls to me while I'm walking with my best friend, Mara, bounding fast down the stairs in a blue nylon running suit and high-tops. I always walk home slow, since my mom is still working at the Silers and on the days I don't go to visit her I like to stretch the time out as long as I can.

"You going home?" Jared asks me.

"No," I say.

For the past few weeks Jared's been trying to walk with me after school. I don't know what I think about Jared. He's old—all the way in twelfth grade—and the other girls say to watch out. He used to go with a girl, Kayla, who has skin the color of boiled tea, twined purple dreads that bounce against her neck, and a proud look to her back. But I like the way Jared tilts his head to the side every time he talks to me. He's got to be mixed too, 'cause his eyes are a gold-green and his hair is a light, fuzzy cap. His face is sharp and pointy like a fox and he's got a long nose, same as mine. I've heard he runs track, and he always wears a nice clean blue nylon suit that swishes when he walks, and always holds open the swinging doors for the teachers.

"Where you go if you don't go home?"

I shrug. "Places." I don't tell people that sometimes I visit my mom at her job; they think it's a little weird the way she's so close to the families she works for, and how I tag along. Up here it's just me and my mama, so I stay close to her.

"You want to hang some?" Jared asks me. "I got a car."

I hesitate, pushing my sneaker into the ground. I think about the apartment: the blinds drawn tight, the big television, the only sound the sirens going by. Sometimes I turn on cable and watch the Indian movies—I like the ladies; they're so pretty, with dainty figures, and they dance and sing those funny songs.

My mom wouldn't like me going with Jared. She's always saying watch out for those boys at school, especially the black boys who are born here. "They aren't taught their pleases and thank-yous, the way we are in the islands," she tells me. "I went for your father, Indian or no, because his mother taught him how to be right with a girl. He never brought me no shame."

Mama's got her ways, like a lot of people from back home. And she don't see there's all kinds here. Yeah, there's some tough guys at our school driving they cars with the radio booming, and sometimes I see Jared with them. But there's also something different about Jared: It's like he's got a little light that switches on behind his eyes, glows from the inside out. He may run with a fast crowd, but he's got his gaze on someplace far off.

"Okay," I say now.

He touches my chin with his finger, lightly.

Marina Budhos

That day Jared and I drive down Springfield Avenue and pick up some gas and then we go get some burgers to eat. Jared likes to play his music loud, so the floor rumbles under my feet. The sky outside is a streaky pink-violet color and it makes me think of the flamingos when they rise up out of the bushes, not far from Grandma Ida's house. Used to be my mother would send me down to Trinidad every summer, but when I got big she said it was too much money and anyway I could take care of myself.

Now, Jared keeps driving, until the lights wink on and the road is dark and by now he's got one hand on the wheel and another on mine. "I don't know what it is," he keeps saying, "but there's something different about you."

"Like what?"

He shrugs. "You kinda quiet. Keep yourself apart. The girls say you got attitude, but I think you just different." He taps his chest. "Same as me. People judge me by all the wrong things, like my sneakers or how I dress. But that stuff don't mean nothing."

Jared brings me back to my apartment house, and he's all polite, hurrying around the other side to open the door, helping me with my backpack. He sure knows his pleases and thank-yous, and when he leans over to kiss me, I'm surprised because all he does is brush my cheek. "'Bye, princess," he says, before bounding back to the car, and I feel as if there's stars bursting in my head as I think, How does he know?

The next few weeks I don't go to my mama's job much at all. I don't know what to think anymore, and what to tell my mother. She always wants to know if a boy goes to church or if he's from the islands or where he's going to college. "We came to this country to better ourselves, Jemma, and don't forget it," she says.

Jared never talks about things like college or classes or jobs. But the more I hang with Jared, the more I learn about him, how when he moved up from Florida to Jersey City all the time everyone thought he was Puerto Rican 'cause of his light skin and they give him a hard time. He learned to walk and act a way so no one bother him too much. "You gotta do some things to get by," he says. "But that isn't who you are." For a while, he ran with the wrong crowd, just to fit in, until an uncle put him in military school. "I learn to think about what's ahead of me, not what's right in front of my face," he tells me. Now he and his brother Ty have all kinds of plans: They want to open a club one day and make records, mixing pop and hip-hop and soca together.

Most of the boys at school, they don't talk like this. Jared's got discipline: Every day he gets up and does one hundred sit-ups, and he always holds himself with a kind of careful air. You know not to mess with him. Jared even takes me to his big brother Ty's house, where they got a room down in the basement and Ty spins records the old way. Jared shuts the lights, but I can't move from the couch; I'm too shy and I feel like I'm all bones and knees. "Just listen," he whispers. I do, and it's like following this little thread of a beat and then I'm standing up and inside, folded into the space between us. I start to like dancing with Jared, 'cause then it's like every part of him comes to life.

Marina Budhos

The tough boy melts off and he's just Jared, moving through all the sounds. He talks while we spin in the middle of the room, palming my hair by my ears. "How come you got such silky-silk hair?" he asks, grinning. "Where you get that from?"

"My daddy," I say, but I don't say any more. People around here are funny about these things, and I never seen an Indian man and a black girl, like my mom and dad were down in Trinidad. So I stay quiet and shut my eyes, just so I can feel his palm on my head, smoothing me into that place that only he seems to know.

My head on his shoulder, it's like I can see my daddy, walking toward me in his gray overalls. He played cricket, my mother told me, and was a good dancer. That's how they met— at Carnival she went to the tent where the Indian soca music was playing and they danced together and the next day she brought him to church and he sat there, calm as could be, with his hands folded in his lap, and she said she knew even though he partied, he was a good soul and Grandma Ida would not object.

Jared's kissed me many times now, on my cheek, and on my hair and lashes, and then full-out in the car one afternoon with the back of my head pressed hard against the glass, his fingers grabbing my sweater through my wool coat. And then one day in my bedroom—or I should say the *only* bedroom, 'cause my mom sleeps in the living room, on the pullout couch—Jared is stretched out on my bed, letting out a low whistle. "Where you get that from?" he asks.

It's a sari, from my grandmother, a sea blue one with gold trim, that I've laid out between us like a long, shiny stream. "My grandma," I say, but the words come out funny and croaky-like.

"Wow. You cut this up and you could make something real nice, wear it at Jam House."

I push the sari away, since I have a funny, squirmy feeling in my throat. "What's that?"

"It's a club Ty's dee-jayin' at. You and me gonna go dance there." Then he grabs the sari and wraps me in it and kisses me long and slow.

I move under him and I want to tell him about Grandma Rupa and how she gave all this stuff to me, but I don't because every time I want to talk about her or my daddy, something hard comes up in my throat and it's like I can't breathe.

Jared's kissing my neck now and it feels like a kitten nuzzling at my skin. Only this time there's warm shivers trickling down to my belly and something warm spreading under my jeans. I try to remember what my mother told me—that America is a bad place for girls, and that black people here don't respect themselves and spend all their money on brand names—but it feels so good, Jared's weight full on me. He wears cologne like a man, which makes my heart race a little. And he's stripped off his blue running suit jacket and his T-shirt and now I can see his arms and his beautiful golden skin.

"You got some other blood in you?" I tease.

"Cherokee and Irish." He grins, and then it's like I'm swimming in those hazel-green eyes, and that golden skin stretching all around is like a warm beach I've been wanting to lose myself in for such a long, long time.

We an item. That's what Mara calls us. We walk down Irvington High, me with my hand on Jared's arm, he with that

Marina Budhos

little jaunty lift in his step. "You hot, girl," she whispered to me at the lockers the other day. "You see the other girls got nails going down your back?"

I laugh. I don't care. I like that those same girls who used to pull my straight hair now have to step away when Jared and I go past. I see Kayla with them, and her eyes go cold. But he calls me his Indian princess, right in front of them, and touches my hair, my shoulders, my wrists. Everything on me seems made of gold.

One night Mama is staying late at the Silers', making pumpkin stew for Sunday church brunch. I tell her I'm going to sleep over Mara's house, and Jared and I head over to Jam House. It's a Friday night and I'm all dressed up special: I'm wearing a green bodysuit, silver glitter on my eyelids. And I did like Jared said—I cut up one of Grandma Rupa's saris and made myself a sheer little vest with a scarf that floats around my bare arms.

I'm pretty nervous, but the minute we step into Jam House I know everything is going to be okay. The whole room is dark, and blue and red lights sweep over our arms, turning them frosty white and light purple. The music comes from somewhere deep, like a truck booming past in the night, pulsing up from the bottom of my shoes, up into my legs so I can't help but take Jared's hand, and soon we're in the music, in a way I never felt before. On the dance floor there's no eyes to cut me up, no one to say I don't blend. I just move and feel Jared's big hands around my waist and we keep looking for that curve in the sound that takes us far away.

I'm all hot and sweaty, so I push my way to the bar,

where someone nudges a plastic cup with some kind of sweet-tasting punch inside. I drink it, then we dance some more until my throat is parched, so I get myself some more drink. Just as I'm heading to the bar another time, I feel a tug at my elbow and my scarf skims off my neck so fast, it leaves a burn. Some tall guy in a black T-shirt is right in front of me, moving his hips. "You dance good," he whispers, twisting the fabric around his hands. "You gonna tie me up with this?" Behind, I see Kayla and her friends in a tight circle, laughing.

A hot itch crawls all the way from the back of my neck around my cheeks. Next thing I know Jared's pushing the other guy back against the bar and he's yelling into his face. I've never seen him like this—fists locked at his sides, thin nose flared. Suddenly the floor starts to go soft under my feet and a sharp pain kicks up from my belly, pops stars into my eyes. I grab for Jared, but I'm down, doubled over. The next thing I know, I'm outside and the air smacks me like a cold hit of water. I crouch on the ground and my lunch comes up, sour and bubbling. I can feel him mopping up the damp grit around my mouth with something soft. When I look up, I see my vest and scarf, crumpled like a dirty wet flower in his hands.

It's after midnight when I sneak into the apartment. Mama is curled on the sofa in her bathrobe, her hair pinned back in neat rows with bobby pins. That wormy feeling in my stomach reaches down to my knees so it's like I'm standing on rubbery splints.

"I knew it," she whispered. "I told the preacher man you

were getting into trouble and here you are."

"Not 'trouble,'" I tell her. "I was just dancing. Like you and Daddy—"

She cuts me off. "Don't you ever say that." Then she fingers my scarf, hanging damp around my neck. It's ugly as a washrag, smelly with my vomit. Her face goes cool. "You go to bed right now."

"But I need a shower—"

"No," she replies. "You see what's like to sleep in the stink of your own mess."

In my bedroom, I peel off my sweaty bodysuit and pants and lie down on top of my covers in my underwear, shivering, my knees pulled up to my chest. Hearing Mama bang the pots in the kitchen, I have never felt so bad.

When we first came here to America, Mama worked two shifts—she took care of kids during the day and cleaned offices at night—and we lived in Newark in a single room with a hot plate. I often got bored because Mama was away so much, so I'd dress up in my Indian clothes and put on the bangles and ruby-chip earrings and dance around the house.

One day a girl from across the hall got curious. "Where you get all that from?"

"My grandmother!" I told her proudly. "Mama says I'm a princess and that's my dowry."

"You better watch," the girl said. "'Else someone gonna steal that."

The next Monday when I tell Jared I have to go somewhere after school, he hunches a little and pushes his fists into his jeans. "You don't want to see me, baby?" he asks. I shake my head and his mouth goes into a sulky curl. My throat is dry. "My mother. I gotta go see her."

He skulks down the hall. The pack of girls are over by the door, and I can feel their eyes slice into me, sharp and glittering. I don't care. I get on the bus, fast as I can, and take myself to Maplewood.

I love the Silers' house: It's light blue shingle with a red porch, and inside there's thick carpets and pictures on the walls, like nothing I've ever seen. I feel calm at the Silers: I like the way the milky light falls on the kitchen table, and the little clouds of steam on the windows from my mom's cooking. Tyler is always racing around in his fire truck and Zoe, the baby is crawling after him, and the phone is ringing like crazy. Sometimes I think my mother likes it better here, that she thinks this is more her home, since our apartment is so small and quiet and I can't make enough noise to keep her there.

When I come in today, she's mopping the kitchen floor and there's a pot of her curry chicken bubbling on the stove. Mama rarely complains. She's long-legged, light on her feet, with a graceful arch even when she's reaching down to pick up a dirty diaper. Today her face is sweet and smiling. "Welcome back," she greets me, and hugs me tight.

After that I go back every day. The minute last-period bell rings, I hurry down the school steps, push past the girls and over to the bus stop. I try to forget how good it felt to have Jared's hands snug on my hips, the lights of Jam House flashing over our arms as we moved together, or how much I loved listening to him in Ty's basement when he talked about all his plans. I want only to sit at the Silers' kitchen table and be near

Marina Budhos

my mama again, to remember why we're here, all by ourselves.

I spend a whole week like this, until the next Monday, just
as I'm sprinting down the steps, someone grabs my arm. I
swerve around to see Jared's face, bunched dark and hard.
"You avoidin' me."

"No," I say, trying to wriggle free. "I was falling behind on
my schoolwork. And my mother . . ."

He spreads his palms out. "Jemma, just listen to me. I'm
sorry about what happened the other night. No one shoulda
given you that drink. That stuff in the club, it isn't me."

"Oh no?"

"You can't judge a person so quick. What if your ma judge
your daddy that way?"

I pause. It's true what he says. Then Jared cups his hands
around my chin. His voice lowers. "Come on. You know we
was good together."

"No." I put my hands on his arms. I can smell the cologne
that scared and excited me so, and I almost fold myself into
his arms. "Jared, I'm sorry. I just . . . I'm not ready for all this,
that's all."

"Why do you lie to me?" he asks. "You can't even break up
with me for real."

Then he saunters off, hitching up his pants. There's hurt in
his shoulders, but I don't go after him.

It gets worse. The girls are on me, something bad. "You think
you something special, huh? Little brown girl with straight
hair showin' up the brother, huh? Who you think you are?"

"Just let me go," I beg, pressing my books to my chest. I angle through them, but it is all pinches and shoves; my scalp burns needles from where they pull my hair. "Runnin' to your mama?" they taunt. Please, I think, let me go. Let me disappear into my down jacket and be no different. I tie up my hair in a bun, but in math class a girl pokes it with a pencil and starts hissing, "Chinky girl now?"

Today it's cold and there's white clouds skimming over Memorial Park, like ice floes. Inside the Silers' house Mama is looking tired; Zoe is on her hip, bawling away, her nose clogged up, her eyes streaming wet. And Tyler is banging a spoon on the lid of the garbage can. "Some days I don't see how they think I can get it all done." She sighs, then points to a pile of uncut potatoes. "Come on, you do those."

As the skins fall into the sink, I find myself reaching way back into my memory where I can see my mama and father walking down a dirt road, the sky rose and silver behind them, the palm trees shading their faces. Mama walked as if she was still a girl like me, swinging her hips from side to side, sassy-like and full of laughs. "Don't see many like them," Grandma Rupa used to say. "She may be a Negro, but she got my son's heart and she the one I pray for." Once she even showed me: She drew a five-petal flower in the rice water on her floor and told me she prayed to Ganesh to remove all their obstacles so they would know only happiness.

When my daddy got sick, she wept and made the flowers bigger and offered bananas and yellow mangoes fresh from her tree. But Daddy only got sicker, and they said there was a poison in his brain that made him say bad things, even to my mother about her "Negro church ways."

Marina Budhos

"Jemma, what's the matter with you?" I look up and see that chunks of potato have fallen to my feet, scattered around my sneakers.

"Sorry," I mumble, and scoop them up, just as I see through the window Jared's blue Honda cruising to the curb. Then he's out of the car, keys bunched in his fist. He's got a tense look to his mouth, and my heart is thumping so wildly I throw the potatoes in the sink and go running out the door to the lawn.

"You can't go in there!" I cry.

"Why not?"

"Because my mama, she doesn't like us going together, staying out late like that."

He pauses, tips his keys back and forth in his palms. "Your mama's right," he says softly. "I disrespected you, and I come to make my apologies."

At first I'm stunned—I never heard Jared talk like that. Then I can't help myself, I'm furious and the words start popping out of me—about those girls taunting me, about everything he made me do that would make my mama ashamed. He stays quiet the whole time, staring straight at his sneakers. When I'm done, I'm so tired I just want to drop down on the steps.

Mama's come out on the porch, Zoe on her hip. "Jemma!" she calls out sharply. "What's going on there?"

"Mrs. Lal," Jared says, putting his hand out. "I'm Jared Paul and I come to say I'm sorry for the other night. I'm here to meet you properly and ask permission to take your daughter out."

Mama's expression softens a bit, though she doesn't take his hand. Instead she takes in every inch of him: the blue nylon suit and the Nike tie-up sneakers. He's not her idea of the right kind of boy, but there's no denying the shame on his face.

"You know I don't abide you taking my daughter out to clubs."

"Yes, ma'am." His neck crooks down as he gazes at the bottom steps of the porch.

"And I rather you come with us on a Sunday to church before you run around all kinds of places with her."

"I understand."

"My daughter says there's some girls you know making nasty remarks about her Indian blood. I don't abide by that, either. Jemma's father and I, we proud of her and what we are together."

Jared's neck hangs a little lower. "I know, and that's not good what those girls did," he replies.

"All right then. You go now. I'm not saying you can go out with my daughter. But you can pick us up eight thirty on Sunday." She cocks a small grin. "That's *morning,* you know."

Jared grins back. "I be there." But he doesn't leave right away. He looks at me, and his eyes are warm and liquid. "'Bye," I say in a small voice, and watch him move to the car with that little jaunty lift in his walk.

That night I'm cramped on my bed with my social studies book on my knees, the print swimming like tiny black fish on the page. Silently Mama steps in and goes to the dresser, pops open the jewelry box, and comes to sit with me, several gold bangles balanced in her palm. Still quiet, she slides them up my wrists, so they make a light, tinkling noise. "Grandma Rupa gave this to me. She used to say I always after her twenty-two-karat gold but that's okay by her."

"You never talk about Daddy," I say.

"I guess I don't talk about Raj because I'm afraid if I talk too much I'll wear his memory down. And then he'll be gone." She smiles at me, and I see her eyes are wet and full. "You got to remember this about your father, Jemma: He was a good man. I knew that from the minute I saw him. You can see that about a person, no matter where they from."

She leans so close I can see the wrinkles that curve around her mouth. "That boy who came over today. He acts like he's bad on the outside. That's what happens to the boys here—they feel they have to be tough. But I think he's trying to make something good with you."

After Mama leaves my room, I sit in the dark, thinking. I think about my father and Trinidad and how hard it's been to put it all together in my head, like a many-colored puzzle that won't go back. I remember the last time I saw my grandma Rupa: It was shortly before we left for America and I was crouched on the road outside her shop, playing with a stick in the dirt. I could hear my mom pleading in her sweet soft voice, trying to talk to Grandma Rupa. But she just sat there on her wooden chair. Her eyes were dead, like wood knobs. The shop, it didn't look too good—there were broken bottles in her water trench and the sign had fallen off.

My mother shuffled down off the porch and took me by the hand and we started to walk away. "Why we not say good-bye to Grandma Rupa?" I asked.

"I ask for her blessing for our trip, but she say all kinds of crazy things. She tell me it's the Negro side gone and poison her son." My mother shook her head. "Never mind. We know the truth, and that's what we take with us."

As we walked away, my feet dragged on the ground. A flock of birds took off, their wings whistling in the air before they settled again on the branches of a mango tree. I twisted my head around once more, so I could see Grandma Rupa. She was still in her chair, like a shadow that never moved. She didn't call out to me. Not Jemie, or Princess, or nothing. She just sat with her hands in her lap, staring out at us like we were no more than spirits, passing in front of her face.

So I took in my fill, hoping I'd know how to carry my Grandma Rupa inside me and keep walking firm on the road ahead.

That Sunday Jared drives up in his Honda and hurries around the other side to let Mama in, same as he does with me. I never seen him dressed like this: He's wearing a starched white shirt and a tan jacket, chocolate-colored pants. He looks good, all golden and brown, put together. After the service, he eats Mama's stew in the church basement and shows the little guys how to run fast, like in track, with your wrists loose at your sides. On Monday we walk together in the halls, until those girls start to call out at me. "Oh, now you good enough for the brother, Indian girl?" they taunt.

I feel Jared stiffen beside me. "Leave them," I whisper.

But Jared's got us right up by those girls. My insides go ice-cold; I just want the ugliness and rough talk to go away.

Marina Budhos

To my surprise, though, he takes my hand and holds it up in front of them. I see all our colors—his dark tan and my nut-brown skin and the pale undersides and the blond hairs on his arm—mingled together. "That's who we are," he says to them. "And you get used to it."

Then we stride down the hall and get in the car, and go to his brother's basement, where Ty spins records and CDs and we listen to all kinds of music. Jared takes my arm and holds me close, his breath warm and ticklish on my neck, the chop-chop soca rhythm mixing with a hip-hop beat, pulsing beneath our skins, in that deep space where he and I are one. We dance, and it's good, and I can feel my mama and my dad move in the hot tent beside us, like two spirits that come and bathe us in a light made of gold.

MR. RUBEN

by Rita Williams-Garcia

That's my boy, Shaheed, I thought, standing at the board with the chalk in his hand, trying to get Myra's attention. How many times have I told him, he's doing it all wrong? Tickets to the Fordham Prep game, yes. Goofy imitation of Mr. Ruben, no.

Mr. Ruben was the man, as far as Myra was concerned. The man. She didn't come out and say it, but she was geeked.

"As always, class," Shaheed said, "show all of your work for extra credit." He did that thing Mr. Ruben does, scrunched up his face like a jack-o'-lantern. It was funny, because Shaheed, with his big nose and bag-of-bones rack, looked nothing like Mr. Ruben. No one looked like Mr. Ruben. He was a one-of-a-kind guy. Tall, but not too tall; light-complexioned, but not quite white; almost perfectly molded, but in an odd way.

Shaheed didn't know when to quit. The class snirked it up, but Myra wouldn't give Shaheed a side glance. Instead she turned to me. Her face said, *Dee, how are you friends with this?*

"Sha's my boy," I answered aloud.

She turned away. Whatever.

I *whatevered* right back. You don't need a reason to like your friends. If anyone should have known that, it was Myra. Myra was my girl in spite of being a freak. Well, everyone in honors math was a freak, self included, but Myra was a real freak.

I caught Yasmin's gaze on Shaheed and shook my head. It was only a matter of time: Shaheed was still fixed on Myra, while Myra was waiting for Mr. Ruben to gallop through that door. I'd been plotting this triangle since September.

My wants were simple. A ticket to the game and to hook up my two best friends. I could have both A and B if Myra would cooperate. If Shaheed gave up on Myra and moved on to Yasmin, then I'd have to cut Shaheed loose—at least for the time being. Yasmin irritated me, and vice versa. The three of us hanging out together, Yasmin, Shaheed, and me, wouldn't work. But if Myra gave Shaheed a chance, just a chance, I'd have A and B, the best of both worlds.

Shaheed and I got tight over the summer at the Castle Hill Y. We were both CITs—counselors-in-training. Shaheed had always been around, but I'd never noticed him until I found myself surrounded by screaming five-year-olds. Shaheed had things under control. He made us look so good that we were both promoted to junior counselors for next summer. I thought about me and Shaheed for a second, but I was never into the whole boyfriend-girlfriend thing. Too many complications. Shaheed and I were more brother-sister.

The class was really laughing it up. Shaheed's back was to the door when Mr. Ruben came rushing in, his tan face reddish. Mr. Ruben doubled as the gym teacher for the period before this one. He was always five minutes late. Well, Shaheed turned, and almost rammed into Mr. Ruben. Was Shaheed's face cracked! I had to laugh.

Myra kicked me. "See?"

Mr. Ruben might have been an egghead, but he wasn't dumb. He told Shaheed, "Thanks for standing in, Mr. Moore. Now have a seat."

Mr. Ruben took out his attendance book, glanced down at the rows, made a check, then started writing on the board, all in one movement. The second his back was turned, Myra and I eyed each other, noting that his low-cut fuzz was now a clean-shaven head.

Damn, I thought. One more quarter inch of hair—enough for a ripple—and we could have solved the whole mystery of Mr. Ruben and his not-quite-white complexion. I didn't care one way or the other, but Myra wasted at least ten minutes of our gossip time each day obsessing over Mr. Ruben. Was he black, part black, or not even? In the beginning, it was fun trying to check out Mr. Ruben's booty, his lips, his nose and hair texture, to pin down any signs of black blood. Now the game was tired.

Myra wasn't crazy about Mr. Ruben's shaved head, but I thought it suited him. Mr. Ruben couldn't help himself. He was neat. Shirt. Tie. Chinos. Might as well have a clean head.

Myra's hand shot up. "Mr. Ruben."

He continued writing. "Yes, Myra?"

Myra's was always the first voice he heard.

"The bonus problem was a trick problem."

The chalk stopped mid-parenthesis. He turned around with that smile.

"Well, actually, Myra . . ." He stopped himself, then

Rita Williams-Garcia

searched the room. "Anyone else find difficulty with the bonus problem?"

The room hushed. Three months into the semester and Mr. Ruben hadn't figured out that only Myra did those bonus problems.

"Shaheed?"

"Not me, Mr. Ruben," he said coolly. "I didn't have any problem."

Myra turned to him. "What?"

Shaheed finally had Myra's attention. He stared her down, using up every bit of his moment, and said, "That's because the problem couldn't be done."

That's right, Sha. Don't let her punk you.

"Correct response!" Mr. Ruben exclaimed, with a glint of jack-o'-lantern eyes. Seeing that Myra, his shining star, was bent out of shape, he said, "You're both right. I suppose I owe you all an apology. I miscopied the problem onto the board. That last part of the equation should have read, *negative r* to the fourth power times *r* to the fourth power and so on. Extra credit, Shaheed, for finding my error."

"Excuse me?"

"Extra credit for you also, Myra," he added.

Myra couldn't leave well enough alone. "We get the full ten points, right?"

Mr. Ruben laughed at what he knew was typical Myra. Yasmin rolled her eyes.

"Well, technically," Mr. Ruben said, "there was no problem, so I can't reward you with the full ten points."

"But that's not my fault," Myra argued. "I didn't miscopy the problem."

Low, but loud enough to be heard, Yasmin said, "What's the difference?"

Myra was offended. "Are you serious? I don't want two points extra credit, or five points extra credit. That's going to screw up my homework average."

"And make it what, one hundred nine, point eight one?"

This was actually funny to Sha and me. We both knew where Yasmin was coming from.

Mr. Ruben held up his hands to end the madness and reel in his class. "Okay, okay. That's enough," he said. "Here's what we'll do. Solve the same problem tonight—as it should have been copied, with the negative in place. And then you can earn your full ten points."

Myra wasn't satisfied. "Not so fast, Mr. Ruben. You still have to give a bonus problem for tonight so it all averages out."

This was why there was honors math. In the real world, Myra would get her ass kicked on the regular, which meant I'd have to back her up. Why? Because Myra was my girl. That simple.

I knew what Myra's problem was. In nine years of school, she'd never gotten a math problem wrong. Not one. Math came easy to me, also, but it wasn't a part of my life. I just solved the problems. Myra, on the other hand, was a freak. She had to *know* the answer, and wasn't happy until an equation was reduced, factored, or simplified and couldn't be broken down any further. That was Myra's approach to math until last week, when Mr. Ruben introduced us to infinite sets. Infinite sets aren't hard. In fact, they're too easy. The trick is, you have to trust them, and Myra wouldn't do that.

It started last Monday. Class began five minutes late like it usually does, with Mr. Ruben running into the room, out of breath, apologizing. Instead of writing a problem on the board, he said we were going to tackle infinite sets, then gave an example about a hotel with an infinite amount of rooms. That was the trust part—you had to go with it. Anyway, the hotel fills up, but an infinite amount of guests show up looking for rooms. The hotel manager then shuffles the guests to every other room, so guest one moves to room two and room two moves to room four and so on and so on.

Myra almost had a heart attack.

"I don't like infinite sets," she told Mr. Ruben. "They're not real. Infinite rooms and infinite guests! Why have any rooms or any guests? All of this endless moving in and out of infinite rooms. I don't see the point. It just goes on and on and on."

When that Friday came, Myra refused to take the quiz. It was okay, though. With perfect scores, she'd earned a few no-quiz passes. I just never thought she'd ever use one. She pulled out a pass, told Mr. Ruben infinite sets made her sick, and sat down and waited until we were done.

Today's class breezed by—well, what was left of it after we waited all that time settling the bonus problem. When the bell rang, Mr. Ruben called out, "Oh, I'm sorry, but, no Math Club this afternoon."

Like anyone was going to Math Club on the day of the Fordham Prep game. The class was out the door, except for me, Shaheed, and Myra, whose face demanded an explanation.

"I've got tickets to the Garden," Mr. Ruben said, excited like a kid.

"Knicks-Pacers?" Shaheed asked. "You call that a game? Where's your school spirit, Mr. Ruben? Fordham Prep tonight in the gym. Now that's a game."

Shaheed gave me the eye. *Dee. Hook it up already.*

I gave it back. *I'm trying, I'm trying.*

Shaheed fanned out three tickets. You need a ticket to get into the game. After last year's heartbreaker, the entire school was looking forward to the rematch. The principal was so worried about crowd control that he'd limited attendance. You had to be eligible for a ticket, meaning no suspensions, two absences or less, no more than two missing homeworks for the semester. And if you were eligible, like yours truly, but didn't get your ticket in advance, you couldn't get in. I'd started boohooing a couple days ago, when Shaheed came to my rescue. He'd said, "I got you covered, Dee, as long as you get Myra to go."

Neither Mr. Ruben nor Myra knew we were passing sign language back and forth. Mr. Ruben, full of guilt, answered Shaheed, "I know, I know. First I cancel Math Club, then I miss our rivalry with Fordham Prep. But it so happens my favorite brother's in town and he's taking me to the game. In fact, he'll be here to pick me up at three thirty. So you see, I have no choice but to miss the school game and Math Club."

Myra didn't care about Fordham Prep or Knicks-Pacers. "Mr. Ruben," she said. "You shaved your head. Again."

Mr. Ruben shrugged, embarrassed. And he blushed. I made a note to myself to point this out to Myra later. *Get a clue, Myra. Black don't blush.*

Rita Williams-Garcia

Myra wouldn't let it drop. "Why don't you let it grow?"

"It's easier," he said, running his hand around his bald head. "No fuss."

Then Myra said, "Wonder what you'd look like with more hair."

Now I was ill.

"The same," he answered. "Only different."

Shaheed walked out the door with my ticket. I was disgusted and ill. I dragged Myra out into the hall.

"You're stupid," I told her.

"What?"

We went to study hall to hang out until the Fordham Prep game. Myra said she wasn't going to any game, but I knew better. In less than ninety minutes she would be sitting in the bleachers between Shaheed and me.

My homework was finished. I had already done English in Social Studies and Social Studies in Music. Most of Myra's work was also done. Except for math. She saved that to do at home.

"He should let his hair grow," she said.

"Why?"

"So I'll know."

I groaned. Here we go again. "What does it matter, Myra?"

She shrugged. "Like I said. I gotta know."

This had been going on since September. In Myra's sick little mind, she couldn't have a crush on Mr. Ruben unless she knew if he was black or had some black blood.

"If he stopped shaving his head, we could see his hair: Naps if he's black-black. Waves if he's black-white. Or straight if he's white-white. I'm telling you, Dee, that man's black-white."

She was serious about this, like she was serious about

getting full credit for her bonus problems. Freak.

We'd been over all of the clues before, but I played with her to pass the time. "The nose is always a giveaway, Myra. And his nose is straight."

"Not straight for a white person," she said. "Straight for a black person."

She had a point.

"Voice," I said. "Mr. Ruben *could* be black by his voice, but then, not necessarily."

"Miss Cutler's black-black," Myra said. "But she doesn't sound black-black."

"Okay. If not voice, he blushes, Myra. Black people don't blush."

She was ready. "Maybe black-black people don't blush, but black-white people do. Dee, he's got some blood; I know he does. It's November. If that was a summer tan it'd'a been faded by now."

Myra had an answer for everything, meaning she spent too much time on the Mr. Ruben mystery.

"True," I said. "But tan skin doesn't give him black blood. He could be 'other.'"

"'Other'?"

"Like you've never seen 'other' on a form? Black, White, Hispanic, Asian, Other. You know how much 'other' there is out there? Look at Joseph. Indian from India. Darker than you and I. Is he black-black? Got black blood? No, Myra. Practically every black-skinned person in this school is from an island. Jamaica. Trinidad. Haiti. Barbados. And the Africans. Don't forget the Africans."

"But they're black," Myra insisted.

Rita Williams-Garcia

I laughed. "Not down-home black-black like us, Myra. Face it. We're the last of the lasts."

"If you have a drop of black blood, then you're black, and I know Mr. Ruben's got a drop. Or two."

"With a name like Ruben?"

The clock hand moved a notch, a reminder that A and B weren't going to happen. Shaheed had probably given Myra's ticket to Yasmin by now. I'd have to sit with him and her—that is, if he'd still give me the ticket.

"So, Mr. Ruben's black and Jewish," Myra decided. "But he's still black."

"Not every Ruben's Jewish," I said, just to mess with her. "Ruben Quinones is Puerto Rican."

Myra was so gone, she didn't know I was playing with her. Instead of sighing, or going *whatever,* she diagrammed her theorem like she was solving a bonus problem. "If Ruben's the first name, then he'd be Latino," she said. "Last name, Jewish. Mr. Ruben. Black and Jewish. Black-white."

I rolled my eyes and thought, Freak.

There we were, wasting time on Mr. Ruben while my precious game ticket was slipping through my fingers.

"This is stupid, Myra. Want to hear why?"

She shook her head no—as if that would stop me.

"You say you can't have a crush on Mr. Ruben unless you know whether he's black or part black, right? News flash, Myra. Number one, you're already crushed, so it don't matter what blood he's got. Number two, you're in the ninth grade and he's your teacher, so where's this going, Myra? Nowhere. Therefore, back to square one: None of it matters."

"It matters," she answered. "In here." She aimed her finger

at her head. Her pointy little head. "Look at him. Mr. Ruben could be anything. Black-black, even."

I laughed at her. "Doubt it."

"Well, I have to know. Black-white. White-white. Black-other. White-other. Other-other. The possibilities just go on and on, driving me crazy."

"You're doing the driving," I told her. "All of this neither-here-nor-there crushing, when you can be going out with Shaheed."

"NO!"

Everyone in study hall looked up. I whispered, "At least you know Shaheed's black and Arab."

"Shaheed is skinny and stupid," she said.

"But he my boy and he cute."

"In a big-nose sort of way."

Myra was weakening—or maybe she heard how dumb she sounded. Black-white. White-other. "You could like Shaheed," I told her, looking up at the clock. Less than one hour to tip-off.

"I did," she admitted. "For a minute."

"What happened?" I asked.

Myra shrugged, but I knew. Jack-o'-lantern head. She was hopeless.

"Tell you what," I said. "If I find out for you, once and for all, what Mr. Ruben is, will you do something for me?"

She looked up, knowing what I wanted.

"Hang with me and Shaheed at the Fordham Prep game. As in, sit with him, talk with him, be nice to him."

"I don't know," she said.

"Aw, give the boy a chance, Myra," I pleaded. "You might remember that you liked him."

Rita Williams-Garcia

She wasn't trying to remember that. "Past tense."

"Please, please, please, Myra. Just one chance."

She closed her eyes, contemplating. I had her. I knew it.

"I swear, Dee, if he makes me ill, I'll leave you sitting with him."

Girl, please. Once I'm up in those bleachers I won't care.

"Deal," I said.

She stuffed her notebook in her backpack. "How will you do it? You can't come out and ask Mr. Ruben what he is, Dee. I can see you now. 'Mr. Ruben, you got some black blood or what?' No. You can't do that!" She was hyper, like Mr. Ruben was about his Knicks ticket.

"Will you calm down?"

I made it clear I wouldn't say another word until she sat still and shut up. When I was convinced she wasn't going to squeal or anything, I said, "Hair."

She didn't have a clue.

"I am a firm believer in hair," I explained. "Hair will tell the story. His brother's coming to pick him up, right?"

She nodded.

"We'll know by his hair. Naps, waves, straight. Dreads. He could be a dready, you know."

"You think?"

I nodded. "And chances are, if he's got some black, his brother will be either lighter or darker, but not the same shade. You know how that goes."

She gave me that one. In most black families no one's complexion is the same. Six kids with the same parents and I guarantee, someone's light, someone's dark, and some- one's in between. Like the kids on *The Cosby Show*. Okay, that's TV, but it's the same thing.

"Then you'll know, without a doubt, without a question, what Mr. Ruben is. And more important, you'll be at the game, sitting next to me"—I rubbed it in—"and Shaheed."

"Just once."

"We'll see."

I called Shaheed on his cell to tell him where to meet us and to give him last-minute pointers.

"You get one shot. Don't blow this, Shaheed. I did my part."

He knew what I meant. He had to be the Shaheed I knew, not the one he showed her in class. That meant no corny moves like singing to her, no bringing up Myra's freaky moments, even if he thought they were cute. No bodily noises, and above all, no imitations of Mr. Ruben. "Just turn yourself down a notch, Sha. Come ready. Have Altoids and after-the-game money. How you ditch Yasmin is your problem."

A and B were finally coming together, all because Myra needed to know if Mr. Ruben had a drop of black blood in him. Not that any of it mattered. It wasn't as if they could call each other up and go out. Talk about real versus unreal. At least Shaheed could take her to a game. The movies. And he was my boy.

Mr. Ruben's brother would be picking him up in twenty minutes, so Myra and I were staked out near the school's entrance, facing the teachers' parking lot. We killed time chitchatting about things other than Mr. Ruben, like in the good old days.

Rita Williams-Garcia

When she wasn't being a complete freak, Myra was cool to be with. And pretty. I couldn't blame Shaheed for wanting to get with her.

Anyway, we both got caught up in talking and laughing and stuff, so neither one of us noticed Mr. Ruben coming toward us from the parking lot. We looked at each other, confused by his blank expression as he neared us. Mr. Ruben was a grinner. He'd see you fifty feet away and start grinning. Now, twenty feet away and he was still blank-faced.

"He must have left the school when we were in study hall," I said.

Myra said, "To change his shirt?"

"Well, he *is* a gym teacher. Maybe he had to."

Then Mr. Ruben walked right by us without saying a word.

Of course, Myra was heated. "Mr. Ruben!" she called. How dare he not know her, not give her that goofy jack-o'-lantern smile?

He turned around, smiled sort of jack-o'-lanternish, said, "Hello, ladies," and went inside the building.

We just stood there for a minute, going, *What?* It was all I could do to keep Myra from going in after him. Luckily, she got a grip on herself. For her sake, I hoped she was now through with Mr. Ruben altogether. I knew she was hurt, but I thought, Good. Game over.

We were heading to the gym when the doors opened and Mr. Ruben stepped out. With Mr. Ruben. Myra and I just stood there looking at each other, and at them. At their straightish noses, shirts with ties, chinos, and matching bald heads. It didn't take math smarts or twenty-twenty vision to figure out that they were twins. Identical twins. Myra wanted to say something to Mr. Ruben, but for once, she didn't know where to begin.

I could see her gears turning, so I grabbed her hand and led her away from the pair of grinning jack-o'-lantern heads. "I don't care, Myra. We're going to the game."

Rita Williams-Garcia

Negress

by Marilyn Singer

Negress is late again. She never used to be late. Then again, she never used to be Negress.

Once upon a time—say, four weeks ago—she was still Vonny DeLong. My homegirl, my sistah, my best friend since sixth grade, when we discovered we had ice skating and Madonna in common. Then something happened. I'm not even sure what. All I know is when she went up to Harlem one day to see some exhibit called "Images of Black Women," she was Vonny. And when she came back, she wasn't.

I've been nursing the same iced tea and french fries for forty minutes. I don't have enough money for anything more. It's a good thing the waitress doesn't care. She remembers when she couldn't afford to eat here either.

We're meeting to discuss our piece for Assembly at Alma Alternative High (AAH!). Years ago, the school's first principal came up with a diabolical definition of "well-rounded": All seniors must do some kind of presentation for the entire student body—music, dance, a scene from a play, whatever. No presentation, no diploma. Vonny and I knew from Day 1 we'd do something together. The problem is it's now Day 1325 and so far we've got nothing. On top of that, Vonny, despite smarts, grace, and verbal skill, can't sing, dance, or act a lick. I can't stand being on display and detest public performance of any kind. We're a perfect pair.

I try and focus on my book, *The Color Purple,* Vonny's recommendation. I haven't gotten very far. My taste runs more to Lemony Snicket. So did Vonny's, once. I manage one more page before I hear a rustle and look up. She's here at last.

"Sorry I'm late, Beth."

I don't tell her she should be. Instead I drawl, "Whassup, girlfren?" It's a good impersonation of an uncool white girl trying to be down, which doesn't come hard since I was once one of only three white girls in our middle school class.

She eases her six-foot-one frame onto the seat. Her face is perspiring a little. When I sweat, my skin goes blotchy and my hair seems made of pasta. But sweating only makes her look prettier. "I was having a conversation with Rondel and Obba about which is worse—accepting Anglo sexual myths or rejecting them. Either way you're screwed." She laughs at her pun.

I don't. "Uh-huh," I say.

She's wearing her "jerkin." That's what she calls the caramel-colored leather top, her newest favorite garment. It shows off the tattoo on her upper arm. The tattoo says "Negress," in the most flowery design imaginable. Orchids trail around the letters and a butterfly hovers over the last "s." My mom was horrified when she saw it. She didn't get why someone would wear an "outdated, offensive word" on her arm. Vonny's parents were even more appalled.

"You had to desecrate your body to make a political statement?" said her father. "What happens two, five, ten years from now, when you're embarrassed by it?"

"And when tattoos are as out of fashion as platform shoes," added her mother.

Vonny told them that NOW was important. That her body and her statement were one.

Her parents replied that they should've sent her to a private school with a strict dress code that would cover up her body AND her statement.

And what do I think of the tattoo? I think it's bold, brave, provocative, in-your-face—and I hate it. I don't want to hate it. But I do. It's like a badge or something for a club I can't join. I hate it that the same girl who once declared, "Black, white, brown, yellow, red, we all have the same color blood," now tells everyone who'll listen—and some who won't—that it's time to "pierce the facade of color blindness" in our middle-class Brooklyn neighborhood.

I am color-blind for real. I can't see blue or green. Vonny's always found that both funny and sad. She used to describe colors to me in terms of other senses—the green feel of grass, the blue music of sky. I loved her for that—and for so many other things, not the least of which is her bad luck with guys, which rivals my own. Chris McWilliams is the latest of her not-gonna-happen fantasy romances, a basketball-playing brother who thinks Negress's ancestors were not from Africa, but Mars.

"I really *am* sorry I'm late. I'm also starving," she says, looking around for the waitress. Nothing new there. She can and does eat mass quantities and never gain an ounce. Today she orders a small feast for herself and insists on treating me to chocolate pudding and a second iced tea. The waitress looks at me and I wonder if she's about to ask whether dessert and a beverage is enough of a peace offering. But no, she just wants to know if I would like whipped cream. I would.

We talk about her cat and my dog and Luis, Ricky, and Jordan's new band and Chris McWilliams's new haircut and why chocolate is so much more comforting than vanilla and it's Beth and Vonny like old times again right through the pudding until I say, "Hey, we haven't talked about Assembly."

"Right," she replies. Her eyes light up with sudden fervor. "Well, I've been thinking about that, and I know *exactly* what we can do."

"What?" I ask. I'm not prepared for the sheaf of Web page printouts she pulls from her handbag and thrusts into my hands. The headline on the first page boldly reads, THE HOTTENTOT VENUS.

"The Whatintot Who?" I say, sounding like a bad comic.

"Read it," Vonny urges.

Reluctantly, I scan the first page. It tells the true story of one Saartjie (pronounced *Sarkey*) Baartman of South Africa. A Khoisian woman, she was exhibited in early-nineteenth-century Europe on a rope or in a cage, like a wild animal, as an example of "*la sexualité de la negresse.*" The story is shocking; the cartoonlike drawing on the next page, worse. It shows her standing there, nearly nude, being examined by

192   Marilyn Singer

two soldiers in kilts and two fashionable aristocrats (one, a woman). The spectators' rude remarks on the size and shape of her parts are printed on the picture.

"Vonny, this is disgusting!" I blurt out.

"I know it is," she agrees. "But it explains all those booty-shaking, *voulez-vous* hootchie-kootchie girls on TV, at rock shows, in the movies. They're Saartjie's heirs."

"Huh? That's BS! Those girls CHOOSE to do that!"

"Do they? Well, so did Saartjie—according to her testimony when abolitionists brought her case to court. She even got money for it. But Beth, when is choice really *choice*?"

I don't know the answer. And I don't want to try and figure it out. How did we go from chocolate pudding to this? And anyway, what on earth does it have to do with Assembly? Which is just what I ask Negress.

She gets all excited and has to take a breath before she tells me: "We are going to present a living picture of the Hottentot Venus, with me as Saartjie and Luis, Jordan, Ricky, and you as her spectators."

"Like hell we are!" I declare.

"We'll have slides first, and a tape. In the dark. Saartjie's history. The history of sexual myths . . ."

"Negress . . ."

"Then the lights. Me in a bikini. Flesh-colored. *My* flesh. You know, they used to have a crayon called 'flesh.' Guess what color it was . . ."

"NEGRESS!" The waitress gives me a frown. Two other patrons giggle nervously. I lower my voice to a hiss. "Didn't you hear what I just said? I am NOT doing this thing with you."

"Why not?" She cocks her head and stares at me, puzzled and challenging at the same time.

"Why not? *Why not?* Vonny, how long have we been friends?"

"Fifteen years, three months, two days, eight hours," she raps back.

I almost laugh, but it isn't funny. I don't understand this girl sitting across from me, and for sure she doesn't understand me. "Yeah, and after all this time, you still don't know me at all!" I exclaim. "You want to stand up there making a fool of yourself, go ahead. But don't expect Ms. White Oppressor here to help you do it."

That stops her cold. It stops me cold too. I don't know where it came from. I don't think Vonny sees me that way—do I? Do *I* see me that way?

After a long pause, she says, in a quieter, more reasonable voice, "I do know you, Beth. I know you don't like to be out there. But you've got to do a presentation, same as everyone, and this way you won't have to talk or even look at the audience. . . . And we'll be saying something, something important. . . . Bethie, we'll shake up the school! Lord knows, it needs a shaking. We both said that."

"You said it, Vonny. Not me."

"You agreed."

It's true. I did. But I don't want to be the shaker—I never have. "You're in enough trouble at AAH without doing any shaking," I say. She knows what I mean—she's under probation for arguing with Lawson, her social studies teacher.

"Look, just think about it, Beth. For me."

Which "me"? I want to ask. Vonny or Negress? "Okay. I'll

think about it," I say, and suddenly remember how I have to get home and help with the laundry. I don't even let her walk me out the door.

At home I take one look at the bags under Mom's eyes and decide to do the laundry for real, lugging the heavy basket down five floors to the basement. While it's washing, I think about this thing Vonny wants me to do. She's right—all I'd have to do is stand there. And make a statement. A statement about what? Racism, sexism—things I'm against, right? So why do I still loathe the idea?

I go back to my room and turn on my ancient computer. My modem's slow as molasses, but I finally get online. I stare at the search field for a while. Feeling oddly tense, I type in "Hottentot Venus" and hit "Enter." The screen immediately freezes. "Saved by the crash," I say aloud, with relief. Then I hear the phone ring.

Mom comes in to tell me it's Vonny, and the tension returns.

"Did you think about it?" she asks when I pick up.

"Yeah," I say.

"And?"

"And the answer's still no." I can't resist adding, "That's MY choice."

She's silent for a moment, and I swear she's going to snap, "Aren't you lucky you can make a choice?" But instead, she says, "Well, maybe you don't know enough to make the right one." She doesn't say it in a nasty tone, but it bugs me just the same.

"Look, I've got to get back to the laundry," I tell her, which marks the first time ever I've used funky towels not once but twice as an excuse.

For a whole day she cuts me some slack. But I know Vonny: She's not going to drop this so easily. She'll grab hold of an idea like a suckerhead remora clinging to a shark and ride that thing clear across the Atlantic.

I know I'm in for a hassle when I see her right before gym class, in her regulation green-and-white shorts with the very nonregulation South African flag stitched to the seat, talking animatedly to Luis, Jordan, and Ricky. Chris McWilliams and his crew walk past and cast an amused glance her way. She catches it and pauses to give back a genuine smile. I feel a stab of embarrassment for her, especially when Chris furrows his brow and chews his lip, as if he's working on a difficult concept in physics, then saunters away into the gym. I don't saunter. I scurry. Somehow I play the best game of volleyball in my life—which isn't saying a whole lot because I suck at volleyball—and surprise the teacher, who's got me pegged as a "PEG": a Phys Ed Goof-off. I even stick around afterward to collect balls and put away the net for the incoming dance class, hoping if I lag long enough, Negress will get tired of waiting and go on to math.

My strategy fails. She's still there in the locker room. She's got that keen look in her eyes and she's waving a newspaper clipping in her hand. "Did you see this?" she says.

"Vonny, we'll be late for class," I tell her, not making a move to take the article. "Reingold doesn't care about me, but you're already in enough trouble with Lawson. . . ."

"The hell with Lawson! Look, look, look!" She presses the clipping in my hand.

I sigh and scan the headline: HOTTENTOT VENUS GOES HOME AT LAST. "Damn," I swear. I've had enough of Saartjie Baartman already. But I read it anyway:

> The remains of Saartjie Baartman were returned to South Africa by the French government early Friday morning.
>
> Baartman, a Khoisian woman known as the Hottentot Venus, was exhibited as a sexual freak throughout Europe in the early 1800s. After her death, her preserved genitals and brain were displayed in the Musee d'Homme, in Paris, until 1974, then were retained as property of the museum. The Khoisian people demanded her return. In February, a French act of parliament at last made this possible.
>
> Said South Africa's arts and culture deputy minister, Bridgette Mabandla, "This is an occasion for celebration for people the world over who advocate the respect of human rights and dignity for all people."

"Oh, God!" I wince. Queasiness rises in my throat. This part of Saartjie's story I didn't know.

"Yes! We *have* to do this presentation, Beth! Saartjie's big news again."

"Page twenty-seven of the *Times* doesn't exactly suggest

'big,'" I say tightly, trying to deflect the nausea I'm feeling.

Vonny frowns. She's clearly upset by the article too. "This isn't something to joke about. You think things are so different now? So much better?"

I take a deep breath. "Yes. Yes, I do."

She shakes her head. "You're not looking under the surface. You're not even looking around you. Put yourself in someone else's shoes for a change."

"*For a change*? What's *that* supposed to mean?"

"Wake up, Beth! The world isn't going to get less racist just because you pretend it is."

"YOU wake up!" I hurl. "The truth is Chris McWilliams isn't going to like you better because you pretend he does!"

Vonny shakes her head. "That was low," she says.

It was lower than low. I can't believe I said it. I want to take back the awful words, but now nothing comes out of my mouth.

Vonny turns on her heel and marches away to class. I stand there wondering who or what I am turning into, and why.

It's not hard to avoid Negress after that. She avoids me. Doesn't call. Doesn't wait for me next morning to walk to school. Sits with Stephanie, Shante, Obba, and Rondel at lunch, Luis, Jordan, and Ricky in study hall. At AAH, if you're working on a joint project you're allowed to talk in study hall. From my corner in the back of the room, I can see that Negress is doing most of the talking. I request a library pass and skip outside to sit under a magnolia in the late April sunshine. There are other renegades there too, but nobody talks— at least, not above a whisper.

Marilyn Singer

I open my pack to take out a water bottle. Saartjie Baartman stares blankly at me from that awful drawing. *Saartjie*, I ask silently, *if I don't play your ogler, will Vonny ever be my friend again? If I DO play it, will she be my friend again? Do I WANT her to be my friend again? Whose shoes should I put myself in, Saartjie? I can't fill Vonny's, and she sure as hell can't squeeze into mine. Huh, Saartjie? What do you say, Saartjie? You're not answering me, Saartjie.*

She keeps staring. *Yes I am. You're just not listening,* she replies. Amazing how her voice sounds just like Vonny's.

Over the next week and a half, under the falling blossoms, I manage to finish all of the Alice Walker and half of a Toni Morrison (with a time-out for the latest Harry Potter). No one has given me—or any of the other defectors—detention, sent me to the library, or insisted I return to study hall. We are all orderly out here, studious even, and the powers-that-be leave us alone. I'm starting to like the solitude and lack of conversation, I think, when one spectacularly sunny day Chris McWilliams and his pals appear.

They lean against a wall, passing around a pack of cigarettes, which Chris, to his credit, waves off, talking loud enough for Dean Sanchez to hear up on the second floor.

First it's just b-ball stuff—who fouled what, who slam-dunked whom. I tune them out and focus with difficulty on Pecola, the abused black girl who yearns for blue eyes, and realize with a start that hell, I want blue eyes too. Always have. Not because they're more beautiful—I don't even know what they look like. To me, blue is gray with a glow. But what I've learned from every movie, TV show, magazine, and ad, from Grandma telling Cousin Suzie, "Your eyes are the most marvelous color!"—something she's never said to me— is that the world is clearly a better place if your hair is the color of Iowa corn and your eyes of California sky. I know this is bogus, know it deep down, but it's never stopped the wanting.

And then an unwelcome thought bounces into my head: Why is it worse for a black girl to want to be blue-eyed than a white, brown-eyed Jew? Like a grenade, the question explodes into a gazillion others. I'm overwhelmed with thoughts I don't want to think, feelings I don't want to feel, and I'm damn desperate to talk to the one person who might understand.

"Negress," someone says, and for a moment I wonder if it's me, but no, it's Curtis Knolls, one of Chris's homeboys. "The girl is wack. You hear she was planning to go naked for Assembly till Sanchez stopped it? Said he'd kick her out on her butt." "*What?*" I nearly yell. I'm suddenly furious at Sanchez, at Curtis, at anybody in sight.

"Nekkid? That beanpole's got nothing to show nohow," says Mickey Swann, a big white guy from Louisiana who, by all accounts, is the best power forward AAH's ever had.

They all laugh—except Chris. "Too bad that girl doesn't play ball," he says. It's not even nasty, but for some reason that pisses me off even more.

I see myself standing up, legs shaking in righteous anger—or maybe just because they've fallen asleep—and getting in his face: "What does that mean? Only girls who swish big balls through baskets get your seal of approval? Or girls who are tall and thin are useless unless they play ball? What about girls with big boobs and butts? Are they only good for one thing too? And does this apply equally to black girls and white girls?"

I see and hear all that—in my head. In reality, I don't move or say a thing. I seethe. I'm boiling so hard I turn into vapor. Chris and friends don't notice me at all.

I decide that no one else will notice my absence either, so I float home, knowing Mom will be at work, and condense on my bed. All afternoon I have weird dreams.

I wake up, hollering, from the last one, where I'm dribbling a basketball that turns into a human head, and grab for my clock. Mom will be home in half an hour. Vonny already is. Or should be, unless she and her new friends are concocting a presentation that will get them *all* kicked out of school.

I scramble out of bed, splash some water on my sweaty face, and before I have time to stop myself, sprint the three blocks to her house. I have to ring the bell four times before she answers. She's in overalls, and her hands are covered with dirt.

"Oh. Hello," she says. She's keeping her voice cool, but there's a flash of warm relief in her eyes.

"Tomatoes?" I guess.

"Marigolds."

"Marigolds are originally from Africa." *Thank you, Mr. Bouley, for that useful bit of fifth-grade knowledge.* I wince. This has got to be up there with "Greetings. Did you know George Washington Carver invented the peanut?" or "I've always thought that Duke Ellington can kick Mozart's ass any day." Jeez, I no longer know how to talk to my best friend.

"These are originally from Long Island," Negress replies dryly.

"I'm an idiot," I say.

A little smile plays on her lips. "Come in, idiot." She opens the door.

We go into the backyard. The marigolds, still small, are set in neat circles. In a few months they'll look like cheerleaders' pom-poms. Last year Vonny wore them in her hair. I never did.

She picks up a muddy trowel and begins to wipe it with a rag. "So, where were you today? You disappeared after math."

Not so invisible after all. "I cut," I reply. Her surprised expression gives me a little tickle of pleasure.

"You? Cut? How come?"

"Didn't think anyone would miss me." I say it lightly—don't want her to think I'm feeling sorry for myself.

All she says is "You need the assignments? I can only give you Carney's and Pascal's. You'll have to call Steph or someone else for the others."

Like I don't already know we don't have every class together? Her officiousness annoys me, but I brush aside the irritation and get to why I'm here. "I heard you're in trouble with Sanchez if you do the Hottentot Venus thing."

She grips the trowel as if it were a dagger. "Yeah? How'd you hear that?"

"The way Sanchez must've found out in the first place. People talk."

She hurls the trowel point-down into the flower bed. It reminds me of some old game we tried playing with a chef's knife when we were twelve. Mumblety-peg. Mrs. DeLong made us wash the blade and chop veggies for an hour.

"Damn," Negress swears.

202   Marilyn Singer

"I'm sorry," I say.

"Are you? Are you *really*?" She glares at me.

I glare back. "Yeah. Yeah, I really am."

For once it's Vonny who breaks first. "Okay. Okay," she says in a low voice.

"I've been thinking about Saartjie. I've been thinking about a lot of stuff."

"Like what?"

I shake my head. I don't know where to begin. "Like . . . like who decided blond hair is beautiful, and why? Why not red or black or gray? How come huge butts used to be sexy and now they're not? And why . . . why . . ." I stop myself. There's a tick-ticking in my head. Another bomb, waiting to explode.

"Why what?" Negress urges, her eyes serious, concerned.

I shake my head again. "Forget it."

"No. Tell me. Why what?"

I take a deep breath and look around her pleasant garden and up the back of the fine house where she lives with her two loving parents. I think of the small apartment Mom and I share—the one we squeezed into after Dad left. I take in Negress's beautiful face and her figure, elegant even in overalls, then glance down at my own slightly overweight thighs and grubby sneakers. I inhale again. *Tick, tick.* "Why are *you* allowed to be angrier than I am?" *Boom!*

I wait for her to pitch a fit or pitch me out. Instead, she looks straight at me and says, "You get to own your anger, Beth, and I get to own mine—but mine has a longer history behind it, and I closed my eyes to it. That history is part of me, and when *I'm* history, I want to have left something behind to show I understood.

I'm sorry if that makes you uncomfortable. I *really* am. But things change. People change. Sometimes they can't change together. But sometimes, Beth, sometimes they *can*."

I don't know if it's what she said or how passionately she said it, but a chill goes down my spine.

We talk all afternoon and into the evening, about anger, history, money, power, skin, blood, heart, soul, sisterhood. It's nearly time for me to go when it hits me—what to do about Assembly and how to salute Saartjie Baartman in a way she's never been saluted before.

During the next few days we get our act together, no pun intended. We cajole and wangle, buy and borrow, exaggerate and downright lie. We fire Ricky—whose loose lips, it turns out, nearly sank our ship—and replace him with Kenji Okuda. We round up a few other helpers, who have sworn, on pain of Vonny's older brother Tee whupping their asses, they will tell no one about Plan B.

What we are strictly truthful about is that Negress will absolutely, positively, one hundred percent NOT be naked, seminaked, or vaguely naked on stage. That is Sanchez's fixation. He gives the rest of our proposal a cursory glance and approves it. The Assembly Committee is more thorough. They actually read the thing closely ("A presentation of the intersection of European and African history as shown through precinematic entertainment exemplifying the objectified female 'Other'") before they too forbid any Negress nudity, then say okay.

Now Assembly Day is here at last. We sit in the audience

Marilyn Singer

watching the presentations that come before ours. Both Negress and I are in old-fashioned dresses and hats. Luis, Jordan, and Kenji are also in costume. Sanchez and the whole Assembly Committee beam approval. Chris and his crew cast curious (and, in some cases, disappointed) looks at us. Obba, Shante, and Stephanie are poker-faced, but Rondel is fighting the giggles. I throw him a stern glance and ruin it with a loud belch. I hope that I don't puke for the fourth time today.

Later I will not be able to remember a single other performance. I'm too terrified to concentrate on any of them. I have never used drugs, but at this moment if someone offered to shoot me with a horse tranquilizer, I wouldn't say no.

Ten minutes before we are to perform, Vonny takes me by the arm and leads me to the prop room to do our makeup. No one else is in there—which is just what we want. I'm shaking like a Chihuahua in the arctic.

"You sure you want to do this?" she asks.

"I'm s-sure I DON'T want to d-do this," I chatter.

"I mean, we can go back to Plan A."

"And get you expelled? I d-don't think so."

"We may BOTH get expelled."

"Uh-uh. We're not doing anything we promised not to do. We're approved. In writing. Your dad's a lawyer. Ask him." I don't know why I'm arguing. She's giving me an out and I won't even take it.

Kenji sticks his head in the room. We jump and scream. "Hurry," he warns.

We look at each other, nod, slather on our makeup, and rush into the wings.

From the shadows we see the flash of slides, listen to Vonny's voice on tape, hear the muffled murmurs of the audience.

Luis, Jordan, and Kenji rustle past us to take their places on stage. Negress squeezes my hand and follows them. I let out a whimper. My feet are Velcroed to the floor. I rip them free, throw off my dress and bonnet, and stumble out. I manage to mount the little square stool and freeze just as the spotlight hits, reflecting off my flesh-colored bodysuit, my hands, feet, and face—all the color of Saartjie's skin. Only my hair, dark and frizzy, is my own.

The audience's sudden silence seems to roll on forever. I stand there so deep in shock, then shame, that I lose myself and have to reach way down to find out who I am. I search out pride and defiance amid the rubble of mortification. I scrounge for power—any power to arouse, to amuse, to offend—in the wreckage of debasement.

Then, right on cue, from the auditorium, Obba yells, "Look at that rump roast!" And Stephanie hollers, "What does she have that I don't?" Rondel sneers, "Good for making babies!" Shante shrieks, "Trollop! Tramp! Ho!" And the crowd goes wild—cheering, cackling, barking, heckling.

Cracking open like an egg, I begin to cry. I look down at Vonny. Her china white makeup is also streaked with tears.

"Come down, Beth," she whispers. "This was a stupid idea. I'm sorry. So sorry. Come down." I can hear her, but I can't move.

"Curtain!" shouts Sanchez. "Drop the curtain!"

Negress reaches out and pulls me off the stand. We are both still crying, but I can feel both our spines begin to strengthen.

Marilyn Singer

"Curtain!" Sanchez hollers again.

Teachers, students, don't know whether to stay or go. There's shoving, booing, laughter. Then we see Chris McWilliams rise to his feet. His friends turn to him, asking, "Whatchu doing, man?" We watch his furrowed brow clear as he starts to clap his hands. Gradually, he's joined by a girl from my French class, a boy from English, then the whole Drama Club. With more speed, other kids, teachers, the custodian, a security guard stand and applaud.

Grasping Negress's white hand in my brown one, I look out at the crowd. In every face, I catch my first glimpse of history. Inside myself, I feel the first taste of something else. I believe the word is "possibilities."

ABOUT THE AUTHORS AND THEIR STORIES

Jess Mowry was born in Mississippi in 1960 and raised in Oakland. In 1988, he began writing stories for and about the kids in his West Oakland neighborhood. Since then, his stories, as well as his essays, have appeared in numerous magazines, anthologies, and newspapers. He has written seven books, which have been published in eight languages, as well as the screenplay for a produced feature-length film based on his best-selling novel, *Way Past Cool*. He helped found a children's refuge in Haiti, works with disadvantaged youth in Oakland, California and mentors young writers. His Web site is: **members.tripod.com/~Timoun/index-2.html**.

On "Phat Acceptance":

In my neighborhood of West Oakland, California—which was also the birthplace of the Black Panther Party during my childhood and early teens—just as in thousands of poor black communities all across America, my friends and peers "smoked, spit, and swore." We also consumed amazing quantities of beer, sweated, smelled bad, and seldom wore shirts in the summer. Some of us were fat and not in the least bashful about it, and few of us had any desire to look like Barbie or Ken. We were also frequently harassed, beaten, and even occasionally murdered by the police—as was one of my best friends, at age fourteen—for the "sin" of our skin color and socioeconomic status.

On the other hand, being of mixed race and able to pass for white if I chose, I often found myself a spy in enemy country, discovering what white kids actually thought about us (black people), including all the enduring myths and misconceptions most white kids learn from their parents and peers. However, it was the ignorance—and sometimes the innocence—of whites in regard to blacks that astounded, frightened, and angered me more than racial slurs, degrading jokes, or the smirking use of the "N-word," and I feel this ignorance is far more damaging to race relations than actual racism itself as professed and practiced by various hate groups.

Many times I've been approached at book readings by white people who were surprised to hear that black kids ride skateboards, build model airplanes, and/or surf the Web. Not surprisingly, many black kids are likewise astonished by black characters who are ship captains, airplane pilots, or truck drivers! It seldom occurs to many black youth that they can, indeed, become these things, because they are offered so few such role models, especially in young adult literature.

I chose to write "Phat Acceptance" from a white character's viewpoint in an effort to show that, even if intelligent and open-minded, most white kids still expect their black counterparts to look and behave as they do in most books, music, or film. In the story, the white protagonist, Brandon, finds that instead of the stereotypical thugger, or at best an underachiever due to both his color and size, the new black boy in school, Travis, is intelligent, articulate, and possibly an artist. Is this "wishful thinking" or "romanticism" on the part of the author, common accusations a black writer faces when his or her characters defy stereotypes? No doubt there are some who will choose to believe that it's one or both of these things, despite the fact that Travis is based on one of my best childhood friends, just as others will question my "qualifications" in writing from a white viewpoint, ignoring the fact that I've lived on both sides of that fence. Additionally, Brandon finds in Bosco the surfer-boy one of those rare individuals who accepts everyone at face value and who was apparently out at sea when the seeds of racism were sowed ashore to take root in the soil of young minds.

Writer and storyteller **Joseph Bruchac** lives in Greenfield Center, New York, with his wife, Carol, in the house where he was raised by his maternal grandparents. Author of more than one hundred books for children and adult readers, he often draws on his Abenaki Indian heritage and the Adirondack Mountain region of northern New York. His Web site is: **josephbruchac.com.**

On "Skins":

One of the most common things heard by a great many Native Americans these days is that they "don't look Indian." Many people seem to expect American Indians to match a certain stereotype—looking pretty much like the Indians in such movies as *Dances with Wolves*. Both my own Abenaki people and others have dealt with that kind of racist perception of what Indians MUST look like. (Although when we dress in full regalia, all of a sudden people say, "Ah, yes, you do look like an Indian.")

Yet even before the coming of Europeans, all Native Americans did not look the same or fit that stereotype. Here in New England, it was not uncommon for Natives to have green eyes, while in the Pacific Northwest, men in a number of tribes often wore mustaches.

Over the last few hundred years, intermarriage has blurred the lines even more. Yet even if they are of "mixed blood," many Native Americans (and their families and tribes) feel it makes them no less Indian. Being Indian is both a cultural and a racial thing. And one of the things seldom talked about is that a great many so-called African Americans (perhaps even a majority of them) have some Native American ancestry.

One of things I have often heard from Native elders is that we must judge people not by how they look or dress, the color of their skin or eyes or hair, but by their actions, by what they have within their hearts.

So, there it is. That is what is behind my story.

And race relations have always been important to me. I have spoken out and stood up throughout my adult life against racism and for treating other human beings with respect. These concerns have influenced me to become involved in the civil rights movement in the mid-sixties, to be a volunteer teacher in West Africa with the Teachers for West Africa program for three years, and to spend eight years as the director of a college program inside a maximum security prison. I will continue to stand up and speak out against racism in whatever form (such as today's trendy Arab-hating) it may take for as long as I have the strength to stand.

Sherri Winston has received numerous nominations for the Pulitzer Prize for Commentary, including her 2003 nomination for work as a lifestyle columnist at the *Sun-Sentinel* in Fort Lauderdale, Florida. In addition to her work as a newspaper journalist, Winston also honored the request of Rosie Magazine to write a feature on the murder of a six-year-old girl by a twelve-year-old boy. She would like to tell you that she leads an active life that includes roller-skating, water-skiing, and hiking, but she'd be lying. While she plans to pursue an active lifestyle one day, for now she enjoys reading YA novels, attending writers' group meetings, and chasing after her two daughters and her two cats for exercise.

On "Snow":

I hope to see an end to color blindness. I find it ridiculous and offensive that someone would have to "look past" my color in order to accept me. We need to embrace stories about race, because they tell the tales of lives, of human beings and how human beings are impacted by color. Such an anthology should weave as many common threads of humanity as it does eclectic strands of ethnicity. And we shouldn't fear that, nor should we be blind to it; we should just accept it, live it, and let it be.

"Snow" came about after years of my witnessing the tensions between black and Caribbean students in area high schools. I grew up in the Midwest, where you were black or white and that was pretty much it. Coming here and living around so many people from so many countries, I began to understand the fine complexities of race. Not everyone who was "brown" was "black." It made me sad to see that the same type of ignorance that black Americans fought for so long, our children were now heaping upon other minorities. I hope "Snow" reminds us that no one is immune to the inhumanity of discrimination and that no one group is any more above it than anyone else.

René Saldaña Jr. teaches creative writing and literature at University of Texas-Pan American in Edinburg, Texas, where he lives with his wife, Tina, and their cat, ISBN. He is the author of *The Jumping Tree,* cited by *Booklist* as one of the year's Top 10 Youth First Novels, and *Finding Our Way.*

On "The Heartbeat of the Soul of the World":

When Marilyn Singer and I met at the American Library Association conference in Atlanta, I had been reading a bit of Faulkner, in particular his novel *The Sound and the Fury* and his short story "A Rose for Emily." So point of view was on my mind. A friend and I had a few discussions about the first-person-plural narrator in "Rose," agreeing that this was an interesting angle for the author to take: Is the POV a spokesperson for the community; the community's consciousness; a singular person afraid to admit his or her singularity and so hiding behind the crowd of onlookers? I've yet to come up with any answers, but this speaker remains one of my favorite narrators because of the ambiguity.

Back then, Marilyn told me that the theme for the anthology was race relations, the stress more on relations between races (that is, the progress we've made; how we get along now) than on the "us vs. them" philosophy. I was listening to jazz, conjunto, the blues, and other kinds of music at the time. And this narrator came alive for me, the first-person plural: we, a collective blues, who knows how people used to get along in south Texas, how they get along now, how they'll get along tomorrow. This narrator, as PD says, knows about the struggle, the suffering—and the overcoming.

@

Naomi Shihab Nye lives in San Antonio, Texas, but her Palestinian father was born and grew up in Jerusalem. Her recent books include *19 Varieties of Gazelle: Poems of the Middle East,* a National Book Award finalist, *Mint Snowball,* and *Baby Radar.* She has edited seven prize-winning anthologies of poetry for young readers. Her novel for teens, *Habibi,* about an Arab-American girl, has been translated and published in Hebrew. She has been a Lannan Fellow, a Guggenheim Fellow, and a Witter Bynner Fellow.

On "Hum":

I wrote "Hum" because I kept thinking about the lives of Arab-American kids in the United States after September 11, 2001, especially those who live in towns or attend schools without many friends who share their ethnicity or mixed identity. I wondered if their lives would be harder. Sometimes I mentioned these thoughts in schools when I spoke to students as a visiting writer. A girl from India told me the lives of ALL immigrants had been deeply affected; she was glad I had brought it up. A blond, blue-eyed boy in Nashville said, "I'm an Arab and no one knows it—maybe after what you said today, I'll TELL."

Also, I have a friend who has a guide dog, and I think those brilliant creatures deserve to be stars of stories from coast to coast. His dog does hum, by the way. Really and truly. I wish the American and Iraqi people could sit in a big circle and hum together. It is a calming note. Same goes for the Palestinians and Israelis. We manage, as human beings, not to think of the simplest things.

○

Ellen Wittlinger grew up in Illinois and graduated from the Iowa Writers' Workshop. Her seven novels for young adults have garnered numerous awards, including a Michael L. Printz Honor Award for *Hard Love,* which also won the Lambda Literary Award. She has two "almost grown" children and has lived in Massachusetts for thirty years. Her Web site is: **ellenwittlinger.com.**

On "Epiphany":

When I thought about doing a story on race relations, the first thing that came to my mind was walking through all those cafeterias with my daughter when she was looking at colleges. Even though the admissions counselor had just told us how "diverse" the campus was, without exception the cafeteria tables were segregated by race.

I was talking to my sister-in-law about this, and she recommended a book to me: *Why Are All the Black Kids Sitting Together in the Cafeteria?* by Beverly Daniel Tatum. The book was fascinating, and I understood what Dr. Tatum had to say about self-segregation being necessary to the identity development of adolescents.

But then I thought, What if there was a white kid who just *wouldn't* give up her best black friend? What would happen? I really wasn't sure when I started writing "Epiphany" whether DeMaris would be allowed to stay at the table or not. But DeMaris just wouldn't take no for an answer.

I can hardly think of a topic more important than race relations. I think the future of this country (and many others) rests on our ability to build bridges between the many races that make America unique. It is a deadly difficult job—one that can't be done only by legislators—and we ignore it at our own peril.

○

Kyoko Mori has published three novels, a book of poetry, and two books of creative nonfiction. Born in Kobe, Japan, in 1957, she moved to the United States in 1977, where she earned a BA from Rockford College and an MA and Ph.D. in English/creative writing from the University of Wisconsin-Milwaukee. She is currently a Briggs-Copeland Lecturer in Creative Writing at Harvard University. Her awards include Best Novel of the Year from the Wisconsin Council of Writers for *Shizuko's Daughter* and for *One Bird* and a Book of Distinction from the Wisconsin Library Association for *Polite Lies,* which was also short-listed for the Martha Albrand prize for creative nonfiction.

On "Black and White":
When I was first asked to write a short story about race relations, I wasn't sure if I could come up with any ideas. The

topic sounded large, political, and complicated. I thought the setting would have to be a racially diverse urban area. I tend to write stories about ordinary people living ordinary, everyday lives. I haven't set any of my stories in racially diverse urban areas, because I've never lived in one, as a teenager or an adult: I grew up in Japan and lived as an adult mostly in Wisconsin, in small to medium-size cities.

I began to realize, though, that race relations is an intimately private as well as a largely political issue—the topic is as much about a character's conflicted feelings about him- or herself as it is about his or her relationships with others of different racial backgrounds. I happened to be working with a character—for an adult novel—who was born in Japan but grew up in a small town in Wisconsin, and I thought maybe writing about her high school years would give me a good topic for the story (and also help me get to know her better along the way). So I wrote the story about the act of vandalism she engages in. That anecdote comes from something my ex-husband actually did as a high school junior in Green Bay, Wisconsin, back in the 1970s. He and his friends hated an old man who used to yell at them for making too much noise, so one Halloween they tarred the old man's fence, and got caught because one of them had dyed his hair green and was easily identifiable. They had to go to juvenile court and pay restitution.

The bird details at the end come from my bird-watching experiences. The white-throated sparrows are just as I describe them—there are two kinds, one with white stripes and the other with tan stripes—but the birds don't seem to notice these differences when they flock or when they choose their mates.

218

The parakeet among the starlings comes from a story another friend told me—about seeing a green parrot flying in a flock of starlings in November. I changed that to a parakeet because I wanted the bird to be a little more fragile. Parrots are hardy birds—a small flock that escaped from cages several years ago now lives in a huge colony in Hyde Park, Chicago, where the temperature gets down to zero in the winter.

Stories are always a kind of collage—made of scraps of things other people have told me, scraps of memories I have, and scraps of things I've made up completely—all the pieces arranged in such a way that I have a hard time remembering, much later, where any given piece originated. In an ideal society, race relations would be like that: all the pieces making a large whole and harmonizing, allowing us to see not only the beauty of the individual pieces, but their differences as well.

M. E. Kerr is a winner of the American Library Association's Margaret A. Edwards Award for her lifetime achievement in writing books for young adults. She has also received the ALAN award from the National Council of Teachers of English, and an honorary Ph.D. in English literature from Long Island University. She lives in East Hampton, New York. Her Web site is: mekerr.com.

On "Hearing Flower":
Latino immigration is transforming the United States, and our small town of East Hampton as well. Our town meetings provide simultaneous presentation in English and Spanish. The sermon boards in front of many of our

churches now announce the subject of the sermon in Spanish and English, and along Montauk Highway, between the villages where one used to find only Chinese take-out restaurants, now we have delis specializing in Mexican food, as well as Cuban and Central and South American delicacies. Discos have Latin nights now, and in the supermarket aisles there are many new foods ordered especially for our Latino residents—some here legally, some not; some documented workers and some undocumented.

My story "Hearing Flower" reflects a little of what is transpiring in my small town. A majority of the workers who come in crews to do house repairs, or who come in twos or threes, are good carpenters, landscapers, whatever. Unfortunately, last summer I had a roof repaired, and what happens in my story truly happened to me. It was an exception, naturally, and it was quickly corrected . . . but like any enterprising writer, I found a way to use it.

Marina Budhos is an award-winning novelist and nonfiction writer who frequently writes about cultural mixture. She is the author of many articles, essays, and reviews, as well as two adult novels and a young adult nonfiction book, *Remix: Conversations with Immigrant Teenagers*. Currently she is working on a young adult novel and a nonfiction book, *Chasing the Dream: Women Immigrants in the New America*. She teaches in the Writing Program at Columbia University. Her Web site is: **marinabudhos.com**.

On "Gold":

This story came to me from the past and the present.

For the past few years, I have been gathering the stories of immigrants: first for my book, *Remix: Conversations with Immigrant Teenagers,* then for a new book about immigrant women, especially those who work as nannies.

And then one day I was chatting with our baby-sitter, who is from Trinidad, and she confided to me that she is half Indian and half black, though no one here in the U.S. ever guesses that about her, and told me how she lost touch with her Indian grandmother, who once owned a shop that sold saris. It was being in my house, where I have many Indian items—curtains made of saris, statues and masks of Indian gods, books about Hinduism—that brought out her hidden background. After that day she began to confide in me about how one of her sons, who looks more Indian perhaps than his brother, is always having a tougher time at school. We live in Maplewood, a quaint suburban town, but nearby are pretty rough towns like Irvington and Orange, where immigrant parents like our baby-sitter are simply doing the best they can.

This story also comes from memory. I, too, am mixed race—half Indian and half Jewish—and when I was around Jemma's age, I had a boyfriend who was black; we used to talk on the phone every night and gave each other "going steady" bracelets. A group of girls from his neighborhood used to stand in the hall or stop me in gym and taunt me, tell me to "stick with my own race"—which, honestly, I wasn't all that sure of.

So I think those old experiences and new stories and voices

melded together in my head. As I was writing, though, I realized that music is one of the ways the kids I interviewed are crisscrossing in ways that are different from when I was growing up.

When I sat down to write my story, there was Jemma and the world she lives in.

◉

Rita Williams-Garcia is the author of five novels and many short stories about contemporary teens of color. Her work has received Coretta Scott King Honor Book and PEN/Norma Klein Awards, in addition to being cited as a Parents' Choice Book and an ALA Best Book for Young Adults. The mother of two daughters, she works full-time for a marketing services company in New York City. She can be reached at: RitaWG@aol.com.

On "Mr. Ruben":

When I was a girl, my black skin defined me as a "colored," "Negro," then "black" person, with a certain history and cultural values—what we now call an African American. Race and ethnic identity have become more complex as more diverse people of color come to the United States. You can't assume every person with black skin is an African American, as you would have thirty years ago.

I am frequently asked by people of color from other countries about my origins. They seem surprised, and sometimes doubtful, when I say I'm African American of Southern parents. I have been a black girl all my life, and now I have to make that clear in some cases. Hmmm.

This fascinates me, this idea of cultural and racial identity. However, there is nothing unique about my experiences. I have a friend who is constantly approached for directions in foreign languages by people of all races. Although proud of his Haitian heritage, he calls himself a citizen of the world. He says everyone recognizes something familiar in his face.

I was riding the subway on my way to work, thinking about the story I would write, when a casually dressed man caught my attention. He was fair-complexioned, but not Caucasian. His eye coloring was hard to discern without gawking, and his hair was cropped very low. There was something very formal about him, even in his casual clothes. I said to myself, "He is not American. He is French-African from Algeria." I started playing a game in my head, imagining his work and interests. I named him Mr. Ruben.

◉

Marilyn Singer has written more than seventy books for children and young adults. Her works include novels, poetry, nature books, picture books, fairy tales, mysteries, and two other short story anthologies: *Stay True: Stories for Strong Girls* and *I Believe in Water: Twelve Brushes with Religion*. She lives in Brooklyn, New York, with her husband and many pets. Please visit her Web site: **marilynsinger.net**.

On "Negress":

Some years ago I saw an article in *The Village Voice* about Saartjie Baartman, the Hottentot Venus, a South African woman displayed like a zoo animal throughout nineteenth-century Europe. She was viewed as a prime specimen of a black woman's sexuality. I was appalled, but also gripped by her story. I couldn't get it out of my head—but I couldn't *do* anything with it either. Not for a long time. And then Vonny DeLong, aka "Negress," started whispering in my head.

I was scared to write about her and Saartjie. How could I, a white Jewish girl from the Bronx, attempt this story? Then Beth, Vonny's friend, appeared. She was scared too—as well as bewildered, angered, and disenfranchised by her friend's emerging racial identification. I made her my narrator. By the story's end, she and I had grown a bit wiser—as well as sadder, braver, and more self-aware. I want us—all of us—to keep on growing.